GLISTER

FURIOUS QUEENS: BOOK ONE

KYRO DEAN

EIGHT MOONS PUBLISHING

This book is dedicated to Philosopher Josh. You're wonderful.

Heirs to the Throne of Ahmar

- *First Heir, Shutor - Killed prior to the Allaedam by Hulon, would have been thirty years of age*

- *Second Heir, Talcum - Killed prior to the Allaedam by Hulon, would have been twenty-seven years of age*

- *Third Heir, Hulon – Twenty-five years of age*

- *Fourth Heir, Nazdael – Twenty-one years of age*

- *Fifth Heir, Bruella – Eighteen years of age*

- *Sixth Heir, Icha – Sixteen years of age*

- *Seventh Heir, Lahmdan - Thirteen years of age*

- *Eight Heir, Qadira -Thirteen years of age*

- *Ninth and Final Heir, Chiba - Five years of age*

CHAPTER ONE

THE ETERNAL WITCH OF SEEDING LIFE

THE YEAR OF THE Seventh Moon's one-thousand-twenty-first Light Pass over Qaf.

She was going to die. There was nothing for it. Not unless the Celestial stars cared for mortal matters.

And they so rarely did.

The witch stared at the purple and white tiles of the throne room, her greasy hair fanning around her trembling frame. Tall columns studded with gems climbed toward a crystal dome that gave a first-hand view of Qaf's swirling cosmos overhead. But the glimmering stars were nothing compared to the shimmering decorations within the palace. Everything from the curtains to the pillows to the guard's lapels was bedazzled in jewels, the queen and her silks most of all. But none of that wealth was for the witch.

In fact, the four weeks she *had* spent in considerable, garish comfort following the queen's summon had shattered into three days of whip-laden torture as soon as the results had come in.

No pregnancy with an heir apparent.

The witch's magic had failed. And now she would die unless the constellations answered her plea.

The floor's cold crept up like vines of an *arak hunak*, stabbing through the witch's skin and seeping deep into her bones. Her heart. Her soul. She wished the dead had already taken her.

"Eh hem."

Queen Qadira's brittle voice sent glass down the witch's spine. The witch looked up, eyelids heavy and a headache pulsing in her temples. The queen walked over with short, bird-like steps in heels faceted like gems. She stopped a shoe's length away, her naturally lavender skin almost too shiny to look at directly. Her glittering robes hung in shimmering shades of white as if she had simply walked out of her gilded palace and through a cloud, only deigning to appear before the djinn of her kingdom so she could step on them.

Queen Qadira looked down at the witch and sneered, her bright red lips gaudy and her eyes burning bright green. "You dare trick Her Radiance, filthy conjurer of inept sperm?"

"Your Highness—"

"Glittering Magnificence," Qadira cut in, her lips as sharp as her tone.

The witch swallowed, choking on the puff of glitter that always surrounded the queen. "Your Glittering Magnificence, my magic is good. You simply need to wai—"

The queen snapped her fingers. Two guards moved off the wall and yanked the witch off the ground so her feet hung limply.

Qadira's thin neck twitched like she wanted to tilt her head to the side but couldn't, her arm-length diamond crown too close to toppling off. The seven large crystals adorning the front winked mockingly.

"You swore on the Celestials that I would be simply glowing by this point. That my fire would be mixed and I would have a child on the way. Vawk!"

She snapped her finger, and her bloodservant appeared, bulbous and raisin purple, at her elbows. A small strip of black hair dusted the very top of his head, while the rest of his body, including his eyebrows, was shaved. His deep black eyes hid all emotion, a useful trait when serving the Queen of Killing. One wrong flicker of color in a djinn's eyes, one emotion that showed anything but reverence for the queen, and it was "off with their head!" The witch was ne'er so lucky. She was sure the purple of sorrow consumed her normally light-pink eyes.

"Vawk, did this walking wench not promise me I'd be blooming with baby by this time?" The queen asked.

Vawk bowed low with a bob of his head. "She did, Qadira."

"Vawk's word is truth. And yet..." The queen bent down and lifted a narrow palm. Bright green fire burst to life in the center, casting eerie shadows along the witch's face that turned her stomach. "No mixing." Qadira's eyes narrowed, and she brought the fire so close to the witch's, the heat and glimmer stung. "My fire is as pure as a lime plucked from the royal orchard."

"Your High—"

The *crack* echoed sharply through the hall.

Qadira had slapped the witch hard enough to turn her head. Pain radiated up the witch's cheeks and split in rivulets across her temples. She blinked back the throbbing pulses. Tears sprung to her eyes.

But no one dared say a word. Not even a startled intake of breath shattered the silence that surrounded the echo of violence. They were all in a cocoon of Queen Qadira's making. A cocoon that choked out anyone who dared want to leave. Who dared speak up. Who dared do anything but inhale glitter and pretend they were happy to be there.

Qadira's words came out as cold and hard as the marble floor. "It's Shimmering Siren of Magnanitudenousness to you, you little cretin. And water is a valuable resource in the cosmos. It's selfish to waste it with your pathetic tears."

"Please!" The witch choked out a sob, sinking lower in the guards' hold. "Please don't kill me. You'll be pregnant soon. It is written in the stars. My magic hasn't failed. Life will grow in you. These things just take time."

"The stars?" Queen Qadira laughed, tossing her hand back and playing flippantly with a crystal earring that hung from her dainty earlobe. "What have I to gain from you or your star? It is either weak and pathetic, or you are for not being able to wield its power. In fact, what have I to gain from any star? My entire council of witches has failed to give me what I want, and they've all called on their precious Celestials as well. But you—" She leaned in close, her neck muscles tight as she balanced her crown, and ran a nail under the witch's chin. "You are the Eternal Witch of Seeding Life, and still nothing grows in my womb. What are stars, then, but shining dots of wasted hope? Our despair only feeds them."

"Do not let them hear you speak so." The witch trembled and glanced up, terror of what the Celestials might do to her temporarily outweighing her fear of the queen. "They are the Bahamut's sisters and not to be mocked."

"Hm." Qadira paused in her fiddling and smirked. "What, pray-tell, do you think a glowing light could do to me?"

The witch went silent, a million terrible answers swirling. Then one crystalized, as loud and clear as the stars in Ursa Major. The answer to her internal pleas, and one that would see her dead.

She begged Pisces in her mind, calling one last time upon the Celestial of Life for a way out, but the answer was clear. Death coated the Crystal Palace. Life would not be given to the queen who ruled it.

"Well? You pathetic bipedal?" Queen Qadira snipped.

The witch twitched and looked up, the answer cutting through her tongue and demanding to be set free. "See inside your broken heart."

The Queen's top lip curled, her eyes flashing white with hints of rage. "Kill her."

Fear streaked through the witch, flooding her muscles with frozen panic. "I am bonded to Pisces. I must fulfill the oath and contract I made when I sought permission to use his immortal power. If you kill me now, the Celestial will come for you and make you complete the terms, instead!"

Qadira smirked and flipped her hand to the side. A dusting of glitter followed its trail. "All the better. I sparkle as brightly as the stars. I might as well add one to my collection."

The witch choked, eyes painfully wide. "You can't trap a celestial being. He will come for you, and make you rue the day you were ever born."

Qadira snapped her fingers once more, and the guards dragged the witch down the hallway. The witch writhed in their grasp and kicked and dug in her heels so they caught in all the lines of the tile. Her screams bounded off the tall ceilings, curses at the cruel stars, at feckless justice, and at the wretched queen.

It was the last she saw of the glistering crown, and the last the moonlight saw of her.

CHAPTER TWO

DEE

THE THIRTY-FIFTH DAY OF *the Seventh Moon's One-Thousandth Shadow Pass over Qaf.*

For a thirteen-year-old girl, there was no greater burden in all of Qaf than having short, slow legs when your twin brother did not. No one was going to convince Dee otherwise.

Her brother raced through the halls of the outer palace in the heart of the City of Pearls, always ahead, looking back at her. Dee's blue, silk harem pants *swished* lightly together as she picked her knees up higher, pushed her muscles harder, and fell further behind. She jumped over a servant scrubbing the floors and past window after window with views of the glistening lake that surrounded the palace and its giant turtles and singing whales.

"Princess Qadira!" her bloodservant huffed from behind, blotches of sweat beading across his nearly bald head and shiny purple skin. "You'll get hurt and break your neck. Slow down!"

She shook her head and glanced over her shoulder. "Not today, Vawk. I can't let Lahm beat me. Not again. Not today."

Desperate to catch up, she dodged through a hidden doorway concealed by thick curtains and down a servant's hall. Several maids screamed as she raced past, and sweat dripped from her bandera and into her belly button. She skidded around a corner and blustered out the other side just as Lahm raced past.

"Lahm!" Dee stumbled over her own feet. "You promised you'd wait for me!"

He didn't look back, skipping down the hall and toward the throne room. She pelted after him, but it made no difference. If she was going to exert this much energy anyway, she may as well cheat. He glanced over his shoulder as he entered the throne room and smirked. Dee clenched her fist. She was going to get him this time.

Clearing her mind, she thought of Lahm and his smug little grin and tugged on her djinn fire. The green smokeless magic surrounded her and pulled her from the spot in a popping flash. The white space between worlds greeted her warmly, but she didn't stay long—she couldn't. She touched a quick foot to the barrier of Ard—the land of capricious humans that shared their world—and bounced back toward Qaf, aiming for Lahm. But she had made a mistake.

The firewalls encasing the throne room forbade anyone from entering or exiting with magic. The magical protections smacked hard against her and shoved her to the closest out-point in the nameless nothing. She managed to find her feet for the landing, reappearing in the palace on the far side of the throne room so she peered in through a set of wide oak doors.

Lahm screeched to a halt before her and blinked. Then he broke out in a guffaw and ran over to her, taking up an easy stroll next to her as they passed by the inner courtyard. Each window held a glimpse of alyasimin and roses, crystal pools and swept cobblestones, and Ahmar's distinct taluli blossoms. Their golden petals and spiked navy vines curled up every inch of brick, tumbling over the edges and into every windowsill as they reached for the celestial.

The light of the First Moon filtered through the openings and played gently in the dark hair of Lahm's ponytail. Nowhere near as long as her waist-length braid, the silky streaks of black often escaped from his cream-colored ribbon. A few thick strands covered his left eye now, and he blew them out of his face, his cheeks a dark purple from the exertion.

He punched her softly in the shoulder. "You forgot about the protections around the throne room, didn't you, shorty?"

"Never." She puckered her lips, rubbing the sting of the firewall's magic from her nose.

"Ohhhh, I believe you," he said with a grin, his tone mocking and playful. Sweat stained the neck and pits of his royal uniform—a tight-fitting purple and silver *murabae* outfit from his earlier practice with the soldiers.

"I didn't!"

Lahm's eyes narrowed before they lit up. He grabbed her arm and dragged her close to the taluli that lined one of the windows. "Say it again."

"Lahm," she groaned.

"If it's true, it won't be a problem." He folded his arms and looked at her with raised brows. "Go ahead."

She bit her lip and glanced between him and the blossoms, knowing if she lied, the taluli would spit their white and sticky liar's milk at her. A useful tool when her ma, the queen, was trying to keep foreign diplomats and local courtiers painfully honest. A terrible one when a thirteen-year-old princess was trying to lie.

"Fine." Dee grimaced and threw up her arms. She had no desire to wear her lies on her sleeve. "I forgot about the stupid magic rules for the palace. It's not like I'm popping in to see Ma while she's sitting on his throne. Children aren't exactly invited to join matters of state."

She stuck out her tongue, and he laughed.

"It was a good effort, even if you tried to cheat." Lahm pulled at his collar a couple of times to cool down. "Next time, if you move your arms back and forth in time with your legs when you run, it will help keep your momentum up and get you going faster. Breathe in through your nose and out through your mouth, and always keep an eye on where you're going."

She couldn't help a smile slipping out to meet his, the sting of humiliation fading with each breath. It used to chafe her, losing all the time. To make her feel like she was not enough. But Lahm never made her feel that way, and being around him was enough, even if it wouldn't be forever. Besides, it was Lahm who stole her toys back when her older sisters, Icha or Bruella, took them from her. And it was Lahm who made her laugh after Hulon pointed out her flaws in front of Ba.

Dee huffed, faking her anger. "You should just be grateful I slopped the pegasi stalls for you this morning, so you could go on your little hunt. Otherwise, I'd be trolloping you."

Lahm breathed out a laugh. "I think you mean walloping me."

Her shoulders tensed, and she put up a defensive grin. "I said what I said."

He shrugged, still laughing. "You can be a trollop if you want. It's no color in my eyes."

Dee studied his face, trying to catch what was funny. What he said held true: no hint of emotion colored his jade-green djinn eyes. No pink of uncertainty or yellow disdain. That was good. But he also lacked the gold of true happiness. All the heirs of Ahmar did.

The thought settled in her throat like a piece of naan she hadn't chewed before swallowing. Lahm always seemed to know more than she did. He could outthink *and* outrun her most days of the week, just like most of her other siblings. The difference was, he was the only one who had always promised to stay by her side.

Lahm set a hand on her shoulder, pulling her back. "Where'd you go, Dee Dee Ra? Stay with me, now. I've got our next challenge ready, one I found on my *little hunt*. We can play this one as a team if you'd like. I know how you hate to lose." He stuck his tongue at her, but his smile was gentle and playful. His jade eyes more closely resembled their father's and eldest brothers' and were a far tamer green than she and her sister's carried.

He grinned and pulled her toward the window, moving vines of taluli for a better view. He drew her eyes to the craggy wall on the opposite side of the courtyard. She followed his finger up the thin cracks, not a single window pocking the surface on the janu'ub side until five stories up, where a small opening the size of a child allowed light to stream into the palace.

"That's where we're headed today."

Dee raised a brow. "Isn't it just the bedchamber for a crazy, old king that was walled up from the inside?"

"So rumors say, but nobody knows." Lahmdan sighed in the wistful way he did when scheming up an adventure. "Imagine the secrets."

Dee's heart beat unsteadily at the thought of such a climb, but she hated to disappoint him. They were two halves of a whole, he a tree and her his shadow. "What if Vawk or Todor catches us?"

"What could they do?" Lahm let out a laugh. "Ring our little necks? They're our bloodservants, they'd just die, too."

Dee pursed her lips. What he said was true. Poor Vawk had been bound to her at a mere fifteen years of age. On the day of her birth, they'd castrated him and placed him by her crib, his life bound to hers but not the other way around. He would die the same way she did, whatever that would turn out to be, though they both were hoping for old age. It was normal. Prudent, even, because it gave the heirs to the Ahmaran throne someone they could trust above all others, and they only got one. But she had always felt a little guilty, especially considering her fate and that of the other heirs to the throne of Ahmar.

Or more precisely, that only one could live to ascend the throne.

She was fairly certain she would never see old age.

Dee sighed and pushed down the squirming in her belly. "Vawk will be furious if he knew I was up to something that could break our necks."

"Then he should have done his job better and not let you wander." Lahm grinned. "You're a bit of a clutz, after all."

She glared. "What about the guards?"

He shrugged, a small shadow falling across his face. "No one's exactly concerned with the collective welfare of the Ahmaran heirs, now are they?"

She puckered her lips and sighed. "No."

"Which is all the more reason we need to see what's inside."

Dee scratched her chin with a dirty nail. "What do you mean?"

"Ma is sick."

"So what?" Dee's chest tightened with the truth of it. "Half the kingdom came down with the *famels* two nights ago, and the royal healers have been at mother's side since the first black spot."

Lahm's normally relaxed face pinched around the edges. "I heard some maids talking this morning after the physician came in. They don't think she'll get better."

Dee stared at him, blinking slowly as she tried to process his words. Ma's sick. Ma's not getting better. Ma's the queen of Ahmar. Ahmar must have a ruler. And there can only be one.

She choked on her spit and looked up at Lahm. "You don't think—"

Lahm curled his fingers into fists on the windowsill. "Ma is dying. The Allaedam is about to begin."

The culling that ensured only one heir lived. Dee's mind swirled over the horror stories of poison and slit throats, of her mother killing her siblings to assume the throne.

"How long do we have?" she managed to squeak.

"A couple of days, a couple of weeks. It's the *famels*, so no one quite knows."

She shook her head, unable to wrap her mind around it. "But we're not ready. All our plans, our promises. I haven't even picked a weapon to learn yet. I was waiting... waiting for one to not feel so awful in my hand. And now I'm out of time. We are." She glanced up at him, heat filling her cheeks. "Are you sure they'll even call it? The Allaedam has never been fought by children before. Maybe they'll wait."

Lahm put his hands on hips, face written with bad news. "Ahmar must have a ruler, Dee. There's no way they will wait on that. Especially when Hulon is already twenty-five."

The cold black of fear darkened her eyes and dampened her fire. "What are we going to do? Where will we hide?"

"There's nowhere that is safe in the palace or the city... except maybe a strange room five stories up that nobody remembers and only a few can fit into," Lahm said with a nod across the courtyard.

Dee swallowed the sticky dryness in her throat. "But our apparation powers. Only Chiba hasn't come into her magic yet. All Icha or Bruella or Hulon needs to do is think of us, and then, *pop*, they're here."

"Exactly, Dee Dee Ra." Lahm patted her shoulder. "Think about it. Not a single djinn has been in that room since it was walled up. Why?"

"Maybe because it belonged to crazy King Malqum who burned all his servants before going mad, and everyone was smart enough to stay away until no one remembered it existed anymore."

"Or maybe it has protections *because* they were King Malqum's, and no one revoked the protections provided to a royal's private bedchambers." He raised his brows and smiled, the blue of hope tinting his eyes.

She hemmed and rubbed at her side.

"Always so skeptical." Lahm laughed. "Even if there are no protections, Hulon or whoever tries to apparate to us will end up in a room they don't know, two to one. Hulon has been studying every inch of the palace since he was old enough to hold a knife. I've caught him in my room thrice after bribing a servant to let him in. He already wears the victory jewels in his crown from Shutor and Talcum's deaths—murders that made him the eldest. If he hadn't been called away as a general to help with Shihala's never-ending Vesparan wars, I bet he would have knocked off the rest of us younger siblings by now. He's desperate for the throne. I'm certain he intends to fix this oversight as soon as the Allaedam is called."

Dee pressed a hand to her stomach with a grimace. It didn't help. She patted her chest and her cheeks, feeling like stab wounds already tore her skin.

"Hulon's a tactician," Lahm continued. "But so am I. And instead of memorizing the same parts of the palace that everyone else does, I want to find places no one has ever been to. And I want you to come with me."

She pulled her eyes away from the tiny, flower-wrapped opening high up in the courtyard and to her brother's shining eyes. Genuine. Caring. Completely un-Ahmaran and her favorite part about him.

"You're giving me your strategy for survival and rule." She shook her head and spoke through the pain in her heart. "That's not strategic at all."

He smiled and yanked gently on a loose strand of her hair. "Or maybe it's the most strategic. We're twins, you and I. Born together, grown together. They housed us together until the age of reason. And during all that time, what did we do but plan to stick together no matter what? So why can't we rule together when the time comes?"

"Because it's never been done before," she said flatly. "Because that's not how the Allaedam works."

"I plan to decree otherwise as soon as we win."

Dee bit her lip and nodded, getting lost in the flower of blue blooming in the center of his jade-green eyes. They had talked about this a thousand times before. About how they would triumph over tradition and rule together. But in those stories, they had been all grown up, not two children who could barely hold a scimitar. The timing was all wrong. Everything was. The shadow that had hung over them their entire lives had suddenly grown arms and hands meant to strangle. But she believed he meant what he said, that he wanted her around, that he would protect her. The taluli blossoms between them swayed, closed, keeping their liar's milk inside.

Lahmdan always told the truth. So she would, too.

"I... I hate the thought of murder and blood," she whispered. "Of hurting my sisters. Even Hulon. I could never wear a jewel in my crown after killing you or any of our siblings. I couldn't. It's why I know I won't survive. I don't know that I want to. You shouldn't waste your time protecting me."

"Waste my time? You're my other half." Lahm set his hand on her shoulder. "Running fast and drinking tea and whatever creepy witch stuff Nazdael does aren't important to me. I need someone who listens, is loyal, and who likes to laugh. I think all of Ahmar needs more of *that*. I don't want to survive without you, and I refuse to rule on my own. Stick with me, and I'll handle the blood. Just stay the good person you are, and that's all I need. So, what do you say?"

She glanced once more to the tiny window across the courtyard, the taluli blossoms still tight-lipped and closed, then looked back at him with a nod. "What do you need me to do?"

Lahm's face broke out in a smile, chasing away the dark. "Let's head down to the courtyard before Vawk and Todor find us. We need to find a safe base camp before the culling starts, or neither of us will make it."

CHAPTER THREE

The Healer

The healer had spent her childhood shadowing her mother's ministrations to the sick and injured across the City of Pearls. She'd spent her intermediate years apprenticing to a crazy but powerful kook. And she'd worked her adult years running her own successful practice as a healer and apothecary. It was far too purposeful a life to wind up dead in Queen Qadira's palace.

The healer squared her shoulder, cleared her throat, and pressed her fingers firmly into the queen's lavender stomach. The royal uterus was tight and small, the size of her fist. Still empty. And still the source of the queen's fury.

"Well?" her Royal Shininess asked, voice cruel. "How big is my baby?"

The healer sighed. "What baby?"

The queen shot up and slammed her bony fist on the table. The painted wood shook, nearly knocking off a blue vase. She seethed, leaning back against the settee in the middle of her opulent bedchambers. "Fix it. Now."

The healer bit her tongue. With how thin and doused in perfumes and glitter the wicked thing was, she shouldn't be considering having a baby at all. Not to mention her dreadful disposition. But the queen wasn't good at listening, just killing those who talked.

"And what would you like me to fix, Majesty? The lack of life inside your womb? Or your temper?" The healer pursed her lips and shook her head. "Neither is helpful for motherhood."

"You ugly, little witch doctor," Queen Qadira seethed. "You dare mock the Ahmaran throne? To make light of its lineage?"

The healer met the queen's lime-green eyes. "What lineage?"

Qadira snarled and slapped the healer with her painted nails.

Pain shot across her vision as white streaks and settled in her temples with an aching throb. The healer gasped and climbed to her feet, spots blurring her vision. Warm stickiness ran down her cheeks, and the faint smell of djinn fire hit her nose as it escaped her blood—tangy and pure and hot. She touched the gashes, then pulled her fingers away, red marring her deeper violet skin.

She would not lose her temper like the queen. She would not react. It would do no good, anyway. Though, perhaps, her tongue had run away from her. She would have to do better if she didn't want to die. For that's what the rumors said had happened to those who had tended to the queen before her. Slit throats, beatings, suffocations, and poison. Everything expected of an Ahmaran queen who was born eighth in a family of nine. Now, it was the healer's turn to try her hand at placating the queen, not that she had had a choice in the matter.

The healer focused her attention on the silky silver bedsheets that adorned Qadira's bed and pulled together periodically under gemmed buttons. Her gaze trailed the intricate patterns woven into the carpet beneath her feet and up the spindle-legged side tables and the olive wood trunk carved with a tree in the corner of the queen's chambers. Every five tiles that lined the floor along the walls, a servant stood at attention, crisp and polished and ready to fulfill the queen's every whim. And in between them, stood guards, ready to kill whoever the queen deemed deserving.

Not her, the healer re-affirmed, sweating at the sight of each soldier's gemstone blade. There would be no reason to kill her. Not with the secret she kept in her bag that could make anyone pregnant.

Composed once more, the healer met the queen's flickering gaze. "My apologies, Your Cunningness. I simply wished to orient myself to the situation. As you well know, I just arrived. So your lack of a child has nothing to do with my skills. Only going forward should you consider the state of your womb my doings. You will not be disappointed again."

She reached into the carpet bag she brought on all her calls to expectant mothers—and desperate queens who wished they were—and pulled out a tincture of pearlescent cream liquid. After a soft shake that sent soothing swirls throughout the glass bottle, she held it out to the queen.

"What is it?" Qadira's sparkling eyes narrowed, each an eerie match to the crystals adorning the tiara that sat daintily upon braided loops of hair. "Rat-pig poison?"

"Mother's Milk."

The queen sneered, a distinct shade of *I-despise-you* yellow coloring her gaze. "What for? I don't have a child, yet. That's your job. You give me a life, or I take yours, that was the deal."

The healer snorted internally. Deal? She had been dragged out of her bed in the middle of the night and forced to wait upon Her Majestic Snippiness under penalty of death. But that was neither here nor there.

She took a slow breath and shook the bottle so the silver swirls churned inside. "It is the milk from a sphinx—the most ferocious mothers in all the worlds—and would do strange things to a djinn child should they drink it. The legends have reported babies growing wings or sprouting a lion's tail or a bird's beak."

The healer tilted her head, noting how sharp the queen's lips were already. "It's a risk for a grown djinn, too, though the side effects are much less severe. Visions, night terrors, unwanted memories. This draught will make you extremely fertile, but expect your mind to wander considerably."

The Queen's cold eyes darted to the olive wood trunk on the far wall. "I have all those things, anyway."

The healer waited for Qadira's eyes to refocus, time stretching long and wide in the silence between. Then it came. The glint of presence in an aware mind.

"Vawk!" the queen snapped.

Her bloodservant appeared from the shadows behind her chair, his head shining in the glimmer of the soft-glow lamps scattered about the room. "Yes, Qadira?"

"Taste this. Make sure it isn't poison."

"It's not—" The queen cut her off with a flick of red nails.

Vawk balked, eyeing the bottle suspiciously. "Your Majesty?"

Qadira eyed him shrewdly, that horrible yellow surfacing once more. "It's you or me. Either way, if it's poison, I'll die. The only thing hanging in the balance is your eternal soul, which will burn if you fail in your duties."

Vawk blanched, the deep purple of his skin paling to a color that almost matched the queen's.

"Oh, forget it, you ninny." Qadira snatched the tincture from the woman's hand, popped the cork, and guzzled it.

"Wait!" The healer and Vawk both gasped and reached for the bottle.

Her Bedazzledness slurped the swirling liquid down to the last drop, finishing it off with a few fist taps on her chest. "Disgusting."

The healer let out an exasperated growl. "There's a time limit on how long that's effective! Do you have the proper mate ready?"

"Proper mate?" Qadira scoffed. "I can have anyone I want. Johann!"

She snapped a finger, and the nearest servant moved from the wall, bowing before her. He had eyes of soft blue and dimples deep enough to fit a pinky finger, not to mention abs that looked more like a brick-laid wall, gold and sparkling above his tight loin cloth. The healer felt the need to look away, and a stronger one to gaze unabashedly at the Jasraib servant Qadira clearly kept for one purpose.

"Sex me," the queen quipped, tossing a leg on the back of the settee.

The healer ground her teeth together. "Mother's milk doesn't work with any male. As with all things Sphinx, there are riddled hoops you must jump through."

"Then what kind of male do I need? Say the word, and he'll be mine." The queen snapped her fingers once more, and Johann dropped to his knees so Her Majesty could prop her feet upon his back.

The healer kept back the twitch on her lips. Or she didn't. She honestly couldn't tell anymore, so infuriating was everything Her Royal Piggishness did. "To conceive, you must have a virile man in his hundred-and-twenties who has thrice conquered five thousand people fill you with his seed when the Fourth Moon has just passed its zenith and Pisces reaches his might in the sky."

"Pisces again. The presumptuous little firefly." Qadira's long nails clicked as she tapped her fingers together, a cold and calculating look in her eyes. "Johann! How long is that from now?"

Johann lifted his bent head, golden curls sproinging. "A thumb's worth of the Seventh Moon's journey across the sky, with just under a month, Your Divine Spectacularness."

Qadira reached up and tugged at a crystal earring hanging from her lobe, twisting and turning it as the glint in her gaze intensified. "Is there anything else I need to know or do to conceive a child with this Milk?"

The tightness in the healer's chest loosened. Perhaps she could finally assure the queen of her skills and move on from this business. Living in the palace for the nine months it took to grow a child would be reprehensible, but the notoriety and fame for birthing a True Heir to Ahmar was nothing to sniffle at.

"I encourage you not to waste this opportunity," she chided the glistering queen. "Mother's Milk is as rare as a *Tabiba* jewel and ten times as hard to procure without losing a limb. I fear you will not get another chance. The bottle you so greedily downed took a human adventurer eight years to find and another eight to answer the sphinx's riddles correctly. And even the milk could not save him from angering the gods and drowning in the depths of an Ardish sea. But so it is with humans. They are as fragile as *paneena* wings. I myself did a great favor for an *effrit* to get that bottle, and it will cost one hundred thousand dinar—a price that is more than generous for Your Illustriousness and which I expect to be paid."

Queen Qadira smiled. "The reward shall be paid to your lineage as soon as the deed is complete." Queen Qadira smiled.

A slip of cold raced down the healer's spine. Her lungs tightened. "My lineage?"

The shimmering queen sat back and stretched, her fingers snapping at the height of her arch.

Before the healer could breathe again, the cold Sapphire of a royal Ahmaran knife slit her throat.

CHAPTER FOUR

Dee

Dee stared up at the window five stories high, her neck craning all the way back, so the single emerald on her headband clicked against her forehead. The First Moon shone brightly in her eyes from where it rested overhead, causing the golden taluli to glow iridescent in its rusty light. The serenity of the courtyard didn't make the climb look any less deadly.

"You sure about this?"

"I'm sure I'm not dying if an Allaedam is called, and neither are you." Lahm smiled, sweat still beading on his light purple skin and pooling on the collar of his uniform.

"And crazy King Malqum's room is your answer to that still, huh?'

"Yep. Now, up we go."

Dee nodded. If she survived to adulthood, it would only be with Lahm. And if that meant climbing a wall, so be it.

But first things first.

She summoned lime-green fire to her fingertips, warm and barely there, like an extension of her voice. Dee looked at Lahm. He nodded. Then she crawled into the purple *yetollamae* bushes that ran along the courtyard's edges. Deep inside the vivid foliage, she scurried her way to the far end of the courtyard to where the river ran under the palace before tumbling out past the walls and into the Crystal Lake. There, she pulled a section of taluli that crept into the tunnel and came out the other side of the palace just below the queen's balcony. She lit her fire once more and held it to the vine, careful not to prick her fingers on its spines. Holding her breath, she watched as the navy stems smoked, withering under the heat.

The fire licked away the remaining moisture, and the stems lit. Slowly at first, the taluli's magic responded with her own and ignited like tinder. Green fire raced down the vines, one lighting the tunnel in a zing of green until it faded into darkness, and the other shooting toward the ground where she stomped it out with her feet.

She waited for the alarm to sound. Lahm had been right when he said the vines would burn to the other side, but when an explosion sounded in the distance, her eyes widened. She curled her fingers to extinguish her flame and raced back through the bushes until she popped out next to him under the window.

"I didn't mean to. I don't know what that explosion was. I lit the vines like we planned and then—"

Lahm smiled and laced his fingers. "Alleyoop?"

"You're not worried?" She eyed him carefully.

"About the shipment of explosive Quwian seeds laid too close to the palace walls that are now lighting with fire?" He winked at her wide eyes. "It's no water on my fire. I've got things to do."

"You didn't!" She gasped, feeling the prick of betrayal. "Why didn't you tell me?"

"To keep you as innocent as possible, Dee Dee Ra. You know how the Allaedam goes. The strongest kill the strongest and then pick off the weak."

"Are you calling me weak?" Her fire flared inside her veins.

"Of course not," he consoled, giving her head a pat, which certainly didn't make her feel better. "You're more than capable. A moon rider, I'm sure of it, silent and shadowy and infinitely good as you wait your turn to catch fire like those seeds. And when you do—" He whistled and winked. "In the meantime, we don't want you to look competent. We want you to look weak so everyone's guard will be down when they approach. And as the youngest besides little Chiba, you're in an excellent position. Who would fear a soft-spoken thirteen-year-old when the next sibling is Icha at sixteen? Now, up you go. Eventually, the whole palace will be streaming with guards, and we'll lose our distraction."

Dee slid her foot into his hands and pushed up, running her fingers frantically over the white stone until they found purchase.

Her stomach sloshed sourly at her twin brother's words. She didn't want to look weak. She had fought her whole life not to look weak because she always was. She'd challenge anyone to anything, hoping she'd find something she was good at. Racing, archery, riding, even useless tea pouring. It didn't matter. She could only do all of it sort of well, none of it supremely. She had even tried her hand at hunting with her father but had never once thrown a javelin, so much she wanted the furry rams to live.

Now, Lahm was saying that was a good thing?

She shook her head and tried to find a toe hold. Her silk shoes slipped and slid over the rock, so she kicked them off.

"Good idea." He smiled, then took a moment to hide them in the bushes before removing and stowing his away, too. Then he jumped up the wall. He scaled the crevices with ease, winking at her as he passed. He was soon high enough, she climbed in his shadow.

Add rock climbing to the list of things she did poorly.

Dee bit back her complaints. Was being weak an asset?

Above her, Lahm made a perilous jump, sending pebbles down into her eyes. She scowled.

It sure didn't feel like it.

Not when compared to the rest of her siblings. To Hulon and his strategies and Nazdael and her magic. To Icha's blade-throwing and Bruella's silky tongue. She was already Lahm's shadow, which left Chiba, who was barely old enough to start lessons. It was easy to *look* weak when that's what she was.

She continued the climb, slipping on looks stone. About halfway up the wall, Dee's arms began to shake.

"I don't think I'm going to make it," she called to him, a quiver in her voice.

"Hold yourself closer to the stone so your muscles have less work to do." Lahm hung from the opening overhead by one arm, waiting for her. "And make sure you push with your legs instead of pulling with your arms whenever possible. They're bigger muscles."

She did as he suggested, and immediate relief coursed through her biceps like the cool of marble on moon-burnt feet.

With the weight off her weaker limbs, Dee soon met Lahm by the window. Sweat beaded on her brow, and her legs shook from exhaustion and knowing she was up so high.

"Ready?" He smiled, and his eyebrows danced. "Fitting through this small window will finally be something your skinny butt is good at."

She scowled and scrunched her nose, wanting to swat him but terrified she'd plummet to her death.

Lahm helped push her through the tiny hole. She squished her shoulders through first, then held her breath when it came to the newly-forming curve of her hips. Success. She fell into a heap that sent dust particles swirling in the stream of moonlight that cut the dark inside the room. He slid in next to her, feet landing gently on the dirty floor and leaving footprints.

It took a moment for her eyes to refocus, but when they did, her heart sank.

She wasn't sure what she had been expecting, but it wasn't this. The large chamber they had crawled into contained nothing but dust. Dust and darkness. Stone lined the floors, the walls, and the ceilings, and that was it. There were no furnishings, no columns, not even old chandeliers dusty on the ceiling or tattered rugs covering the floor. It was simply empty with an opening on each side concealed by a door.

Dee bit her lip and looked at Lahm, who shrugged. They each took a door.

The chamber Dee wandered through seemed to hold nothing at first glance. She lit her palms and cast a green glow about the room. The walls soaked up the light and gave little back, but it was enough to see.

"It's empty," she called to Lahm, disappointment souring her stomach. "There's nothing here."

"Same," Lahm called back. He met her in the room they had crawled into, expression flat and hand in his pocket. He shook his head and narrowed his eyes, which glowed with his sage-green fire. "That's alright. It gives us plenty of space to fill it up."

"With what?"

"Everything we need to win the Allaedam. We can start prepping today. Bring up weapons and food and anything else we need."

"And climb up with all that? I could barely pull myself up with these scrawny arms." She lifted her elbow and sighed.

Lahm laughed, which pricked at her again. "We wouldn't have to worry about that if one of us stayed up here. Then the other one could just apparate up with whatever we need."

She opened her mouth, then shut it as realization dawned on her. "You could have just climbed the wall and had me apparate up."

"That is something that could be true." He nodded with a smile.

"Why did you make me climb, then!"

"Why didn't you think of it yourself? You were the one worried about everyone apparating up here once we made it."

She bristled. "And rightly so."

"Don't be mad, Dee Dee Ra." He laughed again. "I wanted to make sure you could make the climb on your own, you know, just in case."

Just in case... something happened to him and she was on her own.

Dee swallowed the implication in his words and felt all the sicker for it.

She bit her ragged thumbnail. "Should we try it? If we can't come in, we shouldn't be able to apparate out either, right?"

"Usually." Lahm nodded, though the copper of confidence in his normally sparkling eyes took a hit. "But this is an older room and one of a king. I don't know what limitations were put in place. King Malqum was quite the unconfirmed philanderer. Rumors say he always got away with his dalliances because, while he required his courtesans to walk in, they were allowed to apparate out. Something about his wife always finding out and storming in with torches, ready to burn him out. Guess one finally got caught in the end." He laughed uncomfortably and wiped a finger across the stone wall. It came off black, and his laughter died.

Dee stared at him in horror. "Our plan for the Allaedam is to hide in a room of sin and unsanctioned murder?" She clapped her hands together and bowed her head. "The heavens cursed this place with flames once already."

"I think Malqum's wife cursed this place, not the heavens." Playfulness returned to Lahm's smile. "But we didn't make her upset, now did we? Which makes it perfect. Now, shall I be the sacrifice as we test the boundaries? Then, if for some reason I can apparate out but not back in, you won't have to make the climb again."

Dee pouted. He was referring to her weaknesses that were supposed to be strengths, though it was not untrue. She did not want to stay in the impromptu funeral pyre of a crazed king. She also didn't want to be alone. What if something happened while he was gone? What if Malqum's ghost haunted these tombs? She shivered against a sudden burst of cold and felt all the weaker for it. She would have to pull her weight or Lahm might change his mind and leave her behind. If the Allaedam was coming, there were things far worse than a dark room.

She met his eyes and acquiesced. He nodded once. Then disappeared.

Because in the end, he was right.

Above all, she did *not* want to make the climb, again.

CHAPTER FIVE

THE MATCHMAKER

THE MATCHMAKER TWITCHED AS the gears on his Celesteela churned slowly with soft clicks, aligning star patterns with birthdates and locations. Eight gemstone moons spun around the edges, twisting back and forth as various astrological phenomenons matched up. It took patience and skill, but that's why he was the best. Besides, now was no time to take shortcuts or make assumptions. Queen Qadira had been very specific about her needs, and his life rested in the balance.

He had six days to find a coupling for the capricious woman. And a coupling for a queen could only mean marriage and one to someone also of royalty. There were nine kingdoms in Qaf, unless, of course, he counted the destitute colony of human snakes in Fyre—and nobody counted them. That meant eight different governing systems from which to scrape a royal coupling, excluding Ahmar.

Eight kingdoms, that was, and one glaring stipulation: a virile man in his hundred-and-twenties who had thrice conquered five thousand people. Easy, right? Rulers all over Qaf fit that description. The matchmaker scoffed as he sifted through sheets of parchment with royal lineages strewn across them in shimmering blue ink. This may yet be his last coupling.

He moved quickly through the first genealogy. Shihala was out after Qadira's disastrous arranged marriage to the whiny Jahmil Amyr. An obvious failure. Shamptu the Finder's entire family was slaughtered for that terrible match.

The next set contained the scattershot lineage of Ahmar's pale neighbors. Entire chunks were missing from Vespar's line, the true receiver of that country's Gift of

Elm having fallen off the map entirely. What remained of Vespar's princes were all far too dirty and poor to ever be allowed in the City of Pearls. They also despised Ahmar. Never mind Vespar royalty never survived to see their hundred and twenties.

Next, there was the pretentious and highly-selective royalty of Elm. There were certainly hundreds to choose from in that country that were the right age—the inevitable outpouring of offspring for a king who lived for thousands of years and had an insatiable need for courtiers—but none of them had ever conquered anything outside a courtroom. The matchmaker wasn't sure a lawsuit that financially decimated a poor town of five thousand so a prince could build his summer home counted. Actually, he *was* sure. It didn't.

The matchmaker rubbed his eyes and added another ball of his light-purple fire to the orb on his desk.

The next set of lineages was thick. Thick and utterly worthless, like everything else in Western Elm. Half of it looked like it had been scrawled by the gnarled claws of a Marleki in the bloody ink of a dead rodent. Every edge was tattered. Splurts of ink blurred words, and dust and a strange stickiness beset the inner pages. It was no surprise, of course, Western Elm's wild population killed any ruler who branched out past a small serfdom. That created plenty of djinn who had *thrice conquered five thousand*... just not living ones. The longest line of hack shot royalty had only three generations, and the bolded word *faqayd*—deceased— splattered the pages liberally.

Which led the matchmaker to Zabriya—home of a pair of pretty figureheads with a bride price on their daughter's heads that would make the Bahamut seize. They expected the same for their son's bride, which Qadira could afford to pay, but it was no matter. The boy was in his mere sixties and hadn't spent a day outside the palace conquering anything. Their noblemen weren't any better, the closest djinn to a conqueror a young woman who commanded their impressive navy.

Another no. He struck a line through name after name. *No, no, no, no.*

The matchmaker threw his quill, ink sputtering across the next set of papers written in bright-red ink. He grimaced. Izrak—home of the Bloody Queen whose son was a mere babe. Any other royal Izraki lines he could follow? No. The murderous woman had assumed the throne by slinking into the king's chamber, seducing the poor schnook, and murdering him violently as soon as she was pregnant. She walked around in her bloodied nightgown for weeks to remind her new subjects she carried the one True Heir and the only one who was capable of wielding the Izraki gift of Elm they were so dependent on for survival. That, and to remind the nobles she was capable of killing them, too. Then, when the stirrings of rebellion had finally quelled, that's exactly what she did.

The lineage of the next kingdom consisted of one concise sheet of paper with silver names written in calligraphy. Jasraib: a secretive nation with a lineage to match. The paper had been bewitched to only show the name of the current ruler—Sultan Sidi Moussa. Though it made sense, none of his children were heirs to his throne. When the old sultan died, the noble families chose the next ruler from amongst their midst, not from among the dead man's children. Besides, the Great Chamber of Jasraib would never consent to a union between the two kingdoms. They held their noses up as the most pious of nations while Ahmar's largest city, Al Madinat, dragged the title of *Madinat Alkhatiya*—the City of Sin.

The matchmaker tugged on his hair and sighed. That left only one option: a Ghaluman warlord. The kingdom was ostensibly ruled by a single Magnate—Utba ibn Utba, the Chieftain of Chieftains—who was far too young and far too married to be of any use to him. But all the bare-chested, minor chiefs of the warring tribes of Ghaluma traced their descendants through the same ancient royal line and could assume the role of Magnate. They commanded their own armies and constantly vied for control over trade routes, resources, and one another.

Perhaps the matchmaker should have started there, but the Ghalumans were also infamously belligerent. They often made sport of throwing matchmakers into pits with the rabid pigrat *khanaziri*, only agreeing to marriage contracts if they made it out alive.

They never did.

The matchmaker rarely bothered with arranging any nuptials for that moon-burnt country, but he was a dead man if he didn't find a match. The means hardly mattered at this point. Death by pigrats would be far more merciful than anything Queen Qadira could conjure up.

He lowered his pudgy nose and ran a steady finger down the list of chieftains, crossing off the too-old, the too-young, the inexperienced, and the maimed.

He made a note of those who qualified but were married. Disposing of spouses would be tedious, but it was entirely doable.

And then his finger landed on Pardaj Althaani al-Ghaluma, Zaeim al-Shukar. One-hundred-thirty years old. Conqueror of city after city. Twice held the title Magnate of Ghaluma before being toppled. He still boasted sizable lands in the gharb and bahamut sides of the country and came from a very robust line. Even better news, he was seven times widowed.

Maybe Queen Qadira would be lucky number eight.

The matchmaker circled Pardaj's name in heavy black ink, held up the page, and compared it to the sky. Line after line, trace after trace, he matched the stars of the magnate's and others' births with the Celesteela, but no matter what combination or match he tried, suited or not, the answer was clear.

Her union was cursed. The stars were displeased. Queen Qadira should not marry. Anyone. Ever.

But the matchmaker wanted to live.

He gathered his tools and scrolls and shoved them into his tattered bag covered in constellations. Then slung it over his shoulder and hurried out the door.

He didn't have a moment to spare. It was time for a trip to Ghaluma.

CHAPTER SIX

DEE

DEE BIT HER LIP and glanced about the dark room. The Gift of Elm bestowed upon the Ahmaran royalty allowed her and her siblings to do things most other djinn couldn't. Not only could they apparate to a person instead of a place, but they also didn't have to stop in Ard on the way and find a triangle back through.

The Ahmaran palace was the exception.

She had no idea if Lahm would be able to come back into King Malqum's old rooms or what stinging rebuke he might get from the firewalls if there were protections in place that still worked. If they once protected a king's room, the council of witches and warlocks in Ahmar would have been thorough. The purpose of the wall is what made it a gamble. These magic, djinn-made nets were made to catch trespassers between worlds and do anything from bounce djinn back to their original destination to maim their entire body and burned their face off.

Her heart raced. Why hadn't she reminded him of that? She was a terrible strategist. She had no idea how to look to the future, plan ahead, or exploit or avoid pitfalls.

What if her negligence *had* burned her brother's face off? They certainly wouldn't look like twins anymore, and then her similar face would remind him that that was the case forever more. Would he still want to rule with her after that?

She wouldn't.

But she did want to rule with Lahm. She wanted that more than anything, even if it seemed an impossible dream. She had always known she stood no chance of winning the Allaedam on her own. She never won anything and had always struggled to view the Allaedam as something that would be. She told Icha she was beautiful when they had lessons together and waved at Bruella's upturned nose in the hall, though neither ever returned the favor. As soon as her older siblings had left the nursery, they had deemed her fodder they had to dispose of someday. Nazdael, she had never really known. Who did? The tinkle of anklets was the only sound she made as she wafted through the palace walls. Only little Chiba still loved Dee. Chiba and Lahm.

Her stomach twisted, waiting for Lahm's return. How long could it take? She peeked out the window to see if he climbed, but only the moon's shadows crept up the wall.

Dee paced the rooms, glancing outside the window whenever she drew close. The fire outside the king's room had grown, green and blue smoke filling the sky with accusatory billows.

How long had Lahm been planning this day? Enough to get the rare Quwian seeds in place. She wouldn't even know where to begin setting up a ruse like that. Had he always known she'd go along with his plan, or would he have done it without her?

She mulled the questions over in her mind again and again, and while the specific answers changed with each turn, one truth emerged from it all. Lahm *was* a strategist and far better than her. That, and she had been right. She'd never survive without him because that would put her against him. Against Lahm, she'd always lose. She wouldn't want to win against or without him, anyway.

By her third pass of the window, she had ripped the cuticle off each of her fingernails. She needed to distract herself while she waited. Who knew how long she'd be there?

Vawk was probably doing exactly as she did and pacing his bedchambers, awaiting her return, his only comfort being that he still breathed. It was a terrible way to treat another djinn, especially one who had kept her safe since she was a baby, however bungling a job he did at times. She would do better. She had to. Or at least, she would if she survived.

Dee scanned the room, taking in the stonework and layout. It smelled musky and dry, and the burnt walls did little to help her see. She made each step deliberate, counting four hundred and two from one end to the other. On her way back to confirm the number of steps, a glimmer caught her eyes, green as her fire and winking from the center of the room on the left. She directed her fire toward it and spied another faint flicker.

She hesitated, wary of any token that could be left over from Malqum's scandalous days. She knew very little when it came to things of a—she gulped—sexual nature, and the bedchambers of a cursed king seemed like a terrible way to start. Though, for once, her mind didn't race with thoughts of Lahm. It was an immense relief she refused to relinquish. So she approached, step by step, toward the gleam.

A whisper of thoughts caught in the air about her, and she slowed. She bent down and pushed a finger around in what she now realized was soot and ash, not dust. The stud of an earring appeared, then the crystal attached. She lifted it from the black and rubbed one side clean with her thumb.

Her face reflected back in twenty faceted, gem-like mirrors. She brought the jewel closer to her nose and squinted at the brilliance that appeared to shine from inside the stone. Was it glass? The Ghaluman Chieftains were the only ones who could transform the red sands of their desert into magic-infused wonders, like cages that could hold djinn fire and were given as tokens of romance. Is that what illuminated this earring? Had Malqum kept a warlord's princess in his harem? Or had this belonged to an illicit guest? Or the queen?

Dee bit her lip and tried to catch the angle of the glow to make out its color. Unadulterated white. Then held it against her skin.

It warmed.

She glanced around the corners of the room, feeling a need to put it on. To feel its heat on her skin. The whispering grew louder. She wiped the other side of the glass clean, hesitated, then removed one of the many piercings in her right ear.

Her heart pulsed heavily in her chest. Her throat dried, thirsty for anything but water.

She slipped the glass earring into the hole in her ear. The crystalline drop hung low, bumping into her neck in warm brushes. The whispering returned. She listened.

And screamed.

Green smoke filled the room near the window. A dark figure appeared, blocking the moonlight. It rushed for her. She fell back against the wall, then clapped a hand to her chest to keep her heart from escaping. The figure emerged from the shadows.

"Lahm! You nearly scared me to death," she gasped before her face fell. "But you're back! Does that mean—"

"Shhhh." He smashed a hand over her lips.

She yanked back, prying his fingers from her face. "What's going on?"

"Ba—"

Bonehorns blared in the courtyard and throughout all of Ahmar, a hollow, haunting sound that resonated in her heart and that could only mean one thing.

Lahm rushed to the small window and peeked out, the golden taluli offering him cover.

"The Allaedam." Dee could barely breathe.

Lahm nodded and leaned sideways for a cautious look out the window. She raced forward to join him, tripped and stumbled, then fell. Her hands hit his shoulder. He grasped for the edge.

Too late.

Her momentum. His. They pushed him out the window. The pull of the Bahamut did the rest.

She screamed and watched him fall. Slow as the Seventh Moon's crawl through the sky, he turned in mid-air, scrambling for a lifeline, a hand to hold.

He opened his eyes wide, the green completely smothered in the fear's deep black as he fell toward the ground.

She reached for him, useless, her blood screaming in every vein. She shut her eyes. A crunch. A thud. The last of a gurgling scream as his body landed on the hewn stone below.

Her body trembled. Bile rose in her throat.

"Lahm..." She choked on his name. "Lahm!" She forced her eyes open and rushed to the window ledge.

His body lay prostrate below, blood oozing from an unmoving mouth. Not smiling at her. Not grinning. Empty. Empty and lifeless and dripping.

A pair of soldiers racing by turned and came upon the body. She snatched herself back into the room, grateful for the darkness. For the black. She hoped it would eat her soul.

Death, death, death.

The warm earring brushed her frigid skin.

She clutched at her chest, trying to crush her heart, trying to save it. She peered once more, unable to help herself from looking upon the broken body of her brother as hot tears ran down her cheek.

"I didn't mean to," she rasped over and over, though the crowd of people at the bottom of the wall couldn't hear her. Couldn't see that the taluli remained closed.

The djinn gathering around the bushes below the window in the courtyard did see her, though. They stared up at her, jaws hanging open and wide eyes tinted with the black of fear and white of surprise in an awestruck gray.

The screech of the bonehorns ended, and her heart seized.

Ma was dead. Ahmar needed a new ruler. The Allaedam would now commence.

THE ALLAEDAM

RULES FOR THE ASCENDANCY TO THE THRONE OF AHMAR

By the grace and providence of the Celestial Bahamut, the Almighty, on the thirty-fifth day of the Seventh Moon's One-Thousandth Shadow Pass, the Fifteenth Allaedam shall commence to secure the throne of Ahmar against the weak and chaotic.

1. *All True Heirs shall immediately return to the Crystal Palace, from which they are not to emerge unless crowned the new monarch. The Buhayra Ruwarin—or Crystal Lake—is forbidden along with the City of pearls. The palace walls shall be the boundaries for the Allaedam, and any Heir who crosses them before a victor is announced shall be killed on the spot for their cowardice.*

2. *All servants shall vacate the palace grounds immediately upon commencement with the exception of each True Heir's bloodservant if they remain living at the time the Allaedam is called. They may aid their Heir, but not cause harm to the other True Heirs in any way.*

3. *All guards are forbidden to intercede or aid a True Heir in any way, under penalty of death and eternal damnation. They will remain solely to confirm the cullings, announce cullings to the people of Ahmar, and burn the culled True Heirs on the royal funeral pyre.*

4. *All healing potions or other enchantments to prolong life are strictly forbidden and must be removed from the palace grounds.*

5. *All unworthy heirs must be killed and confirmed by Blood Fire to ensure the safety of the Ahmaran throne. Only one Heir can rule.*

FIRST CULLING

A Formal Allaedam Declaration

By the grace and providence of the Celestial Bahamut on the thirty-fifth day of the Seventh Moon's One Thousandth Shadow Pass, in the time of the Fifteenth Allaedam to secure the throne of Ahmar, a culling eliminated the weak and chaotic. During the Allaedam, the Eighth Heir of the True Nine who have claim to the throne of Ahmar killed the Seventh Heir by pushing him out a fifth-story window of the Crystal Palace, causing him to hit the pavement and bleed out from a head wound and many incurable fractures.

The official record of True Heirs to the Ahmaran throne reads as:

First True Heir, Shutor - Honorably killed by the Third Heir for his country

Second True Heir, Talcum - Honorably killed by the Third Heir for his country

Third True Heir, Hulon - Living at 25 years old

Fourth True Heir, Nazdael - Living at 21 years old

Fifth True Heir, Bruella - Living at 18 years old

Sixth True Heir, Icha - Living at 16 years old

Seventh True Heir, Lahmdan - Honorably killed by the Eighth Heir for her country

Eighth True Heir Qadira - Living at 13 years old

Ninth and final True Heir, Chiba - Living at 5 years old

No other deaths are yet recorded as the country awaits the victor of the Allaedam, but with the Bahamut as Ahmar's witness, only one heir can rule.

CHAPTER SEVEN

The King and the Father

Akila had run into the King of Ahmar in the woods outside the City of Pearls, a lovely deciduous forest of purple and blue that drew in the rare *sansaazi* every spring. She had seen these bright yellow birds first on a shopkeeper's passing caravan as a child and found them stunning.

It had taken a life of study and patience to convince her warlord father to let her leave Ghaluma in search of them in the wild—*Your red skin will stand out in a sea of polluted purple*, her father had always said—but she was determined to go. Granted, he had only consented because she had told him she was going to hunt the rare birds down and bring their feathers home as a prize, but the shame of returning home empty-handed was worth the thrill of adventure. Of finding what she had searched for her whole life.

That all changed when King Malqum rode by on a silver-tipped pegasus, his cream-colored kaftan pristine despite the rugged surroundings. He spoke to her then, called her *jamila* and *hakim* and *mahbub*, and laughed deeply and richly at her teasing. She laughed, too, for his grand attention and even grander procession of servants and courtiers who all stood around to watch as if nothing else were more important in all the world. Stunned by her beauty and quietude, Malqum had insisted he follow her through the woods the whole rest of the day. But the moonlight faded into darker woods as she realized his looming intent.

His hands grasped more desperately. His voice became sharper if she strayed too far. And his heavy boots chased away far more than the sansaazi, but she had forgotten about the birds for that brief moment, so grandiose and intimidating was this strange man who had scooped her up from nowhere.

She was intoxicated and terrified. Intrigued and repulsed. And utterly, embarrassingly helpless. He had taken a fancy to her, he had said. She was stunning and radiant—a star on earth. And that was all he needed for permission in the land that was his own. That night, he locked her up in his palace that sat in the middle of a vast and unswimmable lake, and in a show of affection, adorned it in the feathers of the sweet sansaazi.

She had been locked up in a house of death.

She became sullen, wilted, and homesick, for there was no heart in a place that was not her own. Only someone else's hearth. This did not deter the king. He came to visit her nightly, ever mirthful as he made her play his games and then lay with her, always at the end. Didn't she love the curtains woven with her precious bird? The barrettes he clipped into her hair, their dangling ends teasing her face softly? The duvet, which was filled with the precious feather, their beauty hidden in plain white so she could stay warm in a city that never cooled.

Then the young king married for his queen a vindictive woman who hated how he looked at other women, how he touched them. She closed the harem and locked the doors, forbidding any of the courtesans from leaving. But the king needed his little bird. So he found a way to sneak her in and out of his bedchambers. The gifts stopped, though. The little freedom she had to breathe or walk the courtyard. She was either in an ever-shrinking cage or being summoned to the king's chambers. Her status diminished. No one spoke of her presence. She became a shadow.

And her father became ever more enraged, as all good fathers would. He threatened legions, pain, and blood-soaked heads on the streets of Ahmar. But he wasn't a prominent warlord in Ghaluma. He ruled a small portion of the Greater Desert and had nowhere near enough manpower to take on the great Nation of Excess. Instead, he vowed he would obtain her freedom.

Then a letter arrived.

Dearest daughter,

I ache every night thinking of you. I look to the stars hoping they will look upon you and tell me how you are, but they remain ever silent. Until yestermorn.

A desperate man will do desperate things for those he loves most. So instead of watching your fate, I hunted it. Enclosed is a pair of earrings, yin and yang, dark and light, sun and moon, piety and godlessness, punishment and reward. Wear these around your king and decide for yourself the fate he deserves. It will be granted, and you will be free. Just make sure the king pays the price he deserves to satiate the stars.

Your hopeful father,

Watalam

CHAPTER EIGHT

Dee

Dee stumbled back into King Malqum's rooms, unable to bear the accusatory eyes of the servants below. Unable to see the blood spilling from Lahm's sweet lips, the life from his darkening eyes. His legs splayed out in horrific angles. The pool of red forming beneath him on the cobblestones of the palace courtyard, a small halo of red.

The bonehorns blared again. A short triplet of urgent strength. An announcement to all of Qaf that the first culling had been initiated. More horns. The faint trill of eight notes that announced the kill had been committed by the Eighth Heir. Lahmdan's death belonged to Qadira, and she belonged to Jahannam, to the place damned souls lived for eternity. She would be the target of all her siblings now, the bloodthirsty heir everyone saw as a threat.

She was not safe.

She never would be.

Not until she was dead.

And the darkness that followed would be exactly as she deserved.

Lahm's broken image flashed behind her eyelids every time she closed her eyes. Seared her vision every time they opened.

She trembled too much to stand, leaning against the rough stone of the abandoned room as her knees weakened beneath her, only the taluli to keep her company, witnesses to the truth of what she had done—accidentally did.

There would be no repercussions, though. No punishment or reprimands. She would be praised. In their minds, only moments after the Allaedam had been called, she had killed her closest sibling. She would be hailed as a strong potential ruler, just as Lahm had warned her against. Bloodthirsty, maybe, but capable and swift. Both things she clearly was not nor could be. But Ahmar would see her as triumphant, and Hulon would move her up his list.

Dee backed up to hide in the shadows of the room so high up, clutching a hand to her heart. She and Lahm hadn't had time to prepare anything. No weapons, no food, nothing. And what had Lahm been about to tell her? She clenched her jaw to keep back the vomit of her soul from pouring out between her teeth.

What had she done?

She fell to her knees in the soot-filled chambers, her heart racing, and retched. Bitter bile came up, and she spat on the floor.

"I didn't mean to," she whispered again. "Lahm...."

Fat tears rolled down her cheeks. Her body shook, and her fire dwindled, both appalled at the idea that she had lost the only person who loved her, that she had been the one to *kill* that person.

A rustle sounded in her right ear. She darted wide eyes around the room, her trembling now stoked by fear. The Allaedam. Lahm had been able to return to the room. Did that mean all her siblings could? She should leave? Return to her bedchambers? Find Vawk—her bloodservant and the only person left in Qaf who was on her side until she or one of her siblings donned Ma's crown.

Dee dug her nails into the cracks of the floor, blackening them with the soot of past sins. She should burn like Malqum. Or resign herself to a swift death at her siblings' hands so she didn't have to live with her awful guilt. So she didn't have to face every day knowing she'd never see Lahm again. Had his body been dragged away yet?

Morbid curiosity stabbed at her ribs. She crawled forward. Her heart shriveled in her throat, and she raised her head and eyed the courtyard once more.

The crowd had grown, clearly disregarding the rules to vacate the palace as soon as the bonehorns blared so they could get a first-hand glimpse of the Allaedam's carnage. The puddle of blood on the stones beneath Lahm's twisted body had grown too, now an aura of death the entire length of his body. And in the center, his large build and princely Ahmaran armor shining like a beacon—Hulon. Already at the side of their brother. He knelt by Lahm's side, his long general's scimitar strapped neatly at his side. Its green emerald-cast blade and white bone handle contrasted sharply with the blood on his knees.

How had he come so quickly? He was supposed to have been in a meeting with a Jasraib diplomat on the far side of the palace.

Hulon glanced up at her, surprise clear in her elder brother's eyes despite the distance down. Their gazes locked. Then, a cold smile formed on his upturned face. The First Moon's light glinted off his teeth and the two white jewels in his circlet crown. The jewels of two of her three dead brothers, felled before the Allaedam began. The jewel of Lahm belonged to her.

Dee ducked out of sight, black nails clutching at her dress, leaving stains. Long smears like claw marks through tender flesh. Had he apparated to Lahm as soon as the Allaedam was called? Their powers didn't work with the dead. Had Hulon come to kill Lahm and found him at the foot of the tower already dying? Or had he seen what she did from the start? And if so, would he come for her next as Lahm had feared? Did he think her strong when she was at her weakest?

She cowered into a tight ball, wrapping her arms over her head. Hulon would be there any second to cut her down. And she deserved it. She didn't want to rule without Lahm. She couldn't. He was everything, and she nothing without him. Why would she want a throne that killed her family, anyway?

She didn't.

She didn't. She didn't.

She also didn't want death.

Death isn't so bad, words snaked into her ear.

"Yes, it is," she whispered, squeezing her eyes so tightly that stars sparked across her vision.

The dying welcome it. As do often the guilty. The evil deserve it. And believers do not fear it. Who is left but those who don't know who they are? And what good are they to anyone? What good are you, *a frightened little girl in a castle of killers?*

Dee stifled her sobs and looked frantically around the barren, blackened room, realizing in her agony that she spoke, that she was being spoken to, but by whom? The voice had been cold and distant, but crystal clear in her mind, in her ear.

"Who's there?"

Silence.

"What do you want?"

Silence.

Dee clapped her hands together to pray and heard a chuckle. She inhaled sharply and tried to focus on the Bahamut's mercy.

Mercy? The laughter increased. *What do you need mercy for?*

"My sins," she whispered, pulling at her hair and bowing closer to the floor.

What sins?

"Mur—" She choked on the word and spat more yellow bile onto the floor. Her heart thudded in her chest. Her stomach twisted so tightly, it would never unwrinkle. "I killed my brother."

Did not the Ahmaran court declare the Allaedam to prevent unsatisfied heirs—which all unascended heirs are—from causing mischief and war in the land?

Qadira frowned, the salt of her tears bitter on her tongue. She still couldn't see anyone with her. Only the taluli blossoms moved with the wind in the breeze. Soot marred the floor, her footsteps marring the black in return. "How do you know so much about Ahmar? Who are you?"

Does it matter when you don't know who you are? You don't even seem to know your place in the nation you're supposed to rule. As an Heir to the throne of Ahmar, it is your duty to keep the country free from anarchy and future bloodshed.

"Whether my country condones our behavior or is abhorred by it means nothing." Dee bit her lip and sniffed, wiping the slower-flowing tears from her cheeks. "I abhor myself. Lahm is dead, and I will be soon."

Or not.

The remainder of Dee's tears clung to the corner of her eyes, less willing to part and stain her cheeks. She wiped at them with her sleeve and took a breath. Her hair hung sweaty against her neck despite the cool of the room, and the earring she had put on before Lahm arrived nestled warmly against her skin.

She reached an absent hand up to it and brushed her thumb over the glass. Smooth. Hard. And pulsing a gentle white.

Dee cupped it with her palm. Could djinn fire whisper? She didn't think so. But she could have been wrong about what the crystalline cage contained. She clenched the earring, as eager to take it off as she was reluctant to be alone with what she had done.

You can't smother me, you foolish footbearer.

"Footbearer?" Dee's fingers tightened.

You're insulted, the voice chuckled.

"I am... not." Dee ground her teeth, not sure whether she should be offended or not. "I have feet, everyone knows that. I bet it is you who wishes you did, you disembodied voice of a *buklak.*"

The laughter died in an instant. *I do not wish for feet, toed-one. But I do wish for freedom. Agree to let me go. I was not yours to find in the first place.*

The hollowness in Dee's chest stung, but the thought that Hulon would be there any moment to disembowel her left her with a strangely cold apathy. "Who's were you to find?"

Silence.

"Ah." She flicked the earring and gave an empty smirk. "Not so chatty now, creature."

I am no creature, the voice hissed.

"And I am no slave. I'll be dead soon, anyway, and then you'll be buried with me in the dirt and worms to whisper to my corpse for all eternity."

Dramatic, the voice whispered dryly. *And morbid.*

Dee glanced out of the corner of her eye in the direction of the earring. Talking to a being she found in the room of a burned, mad king was a terrible idea, but it was also the only thing keeping her from weeping the tears of the damned and throwing herself out the window after Lahm.

"It is also true," she said each word with careful neutrality. "Now, tell me your name, or I shan't talk to you at all."

The threat of a mortal who knows nothing.

Dee's confidence wavered. How could it not when its source lay crumpled in a bleeding heap five stories down? But Lahm's horrible death and the calling of the Allaedam also came with the promise of nothing to lose.

"You're right, being, I know nothing. We can remedy that with your name."

Names have power. I do not give what is not necessary, and I do not give for free.

Dee rubbed the smooth glass and puckered her lips, thinking, thinking. What could she possibly give when she had lost the only thing that mattered?

"How about a fair exchange then? My name for yours."

My *name for yours?* The voice scoffed. *You offer but a moment to the eternities.*

"I don't see any other offers on your table. As far as I can tell, you've been laying in soot for at least two hundred years. That can't be nothing."

The silence was so palpable, Dee could almost hear the voice squirm.

I am Kakkab, it spoke at last.

A warm chill ran down her spine, both highly unsettling and like a warm bath.

"And I am Princess Qadira, Eighth True Heir to the throne of Ahamar and seventh living heir—er, sixth." The skin around her lips tightened. "But everyone who doesn't want to kill me calls me Dee. Which... is no one, I guess."

Her eyes fell to the soot-covered stone, her heart aching for Lahm and unwilling to think of her five-year-old sister's coming fate. What would Hulon do to such innocent, wide eyes and chubby, young cheeks?

And are you willing to make another deal, Qa-dee-ra who no one calls Dee?

She bit her lip, chewing ferociously. What would Lahm do? Probably throw the earring out the window. But what if this creature was more powerful than she thought? What if someone else found it and Kakkab wanted revenge for the way she treated him? She wasn't sure what he was capable of. If the Allaedam could be called in a couple of days or weeks, she couldn't risk having a vindictive being hunting her in addition to everyone else. He would have to stay put and close by. She would figure out what to do with him later.

"No." She let out a quivering breath. "Not with things I don't understand."

So you will not make a deal to release me? Kakkab's voice shook deep in her brain.

"I do not even know what I release you from or how to do it."

I suffer from a punishment undeserved. Let me assist you in surviving. I will slaughter your enemies and make you queen. In return, you shatter my glass cage and free me.

She scoffed and it felt like her lungs were being scraped clean by a spoon. "Because I believe a creepy voice who whispers of death in my ear."

There's no reason to keep me, you bipedal biodome with barely a brain.

"Until I understand what you are, there's no reason to let you go."

Kakkab hissed. *Then perhaps I will give you one.*

Dee's eyes widened.

Steps slapped on the tile behind her, catching her ear, unwelcome and sinister.

Her heart leaped into her throat.

Someone had found her.

Most likely an accuser come to congratulate her murder of Lahm with a knife in her back. Or worse—a being come to show her just exactly who he was.

Fear clenched her heart, skipping beats and pulsing pain into her palms. She couldn't stay here to die. Not in this place. Not in this way.

She scurried forward and thought of the only person she had left who could help her. Then, she clenched her eyes shut, and apparated in a puff of green smoke.

CHAPTER NINE

THE WARLORD

THE WARLORD PINCHED HIS lips tight, shifting them from one side to the other as he took in the painted image of Queen Qadira's waify figure. Her form, while elegant, was exactly what he expected from a spoiled brat who grew up in Ahmar. He wanted grand swoops and deep curves. A scar or two to show she did more than sit around on a pin cushion and complain about dirt. But all Ahmaran women were the same—godless, vain little creatures with brittle bones and even brittler tempers.

Then said, Ahmar was well-known for its blood-soaked ascendancy to the throne. If he remembered correctly, this Qadira had had several siblings, the most promising of which had been a rising military general and a renowned blade specialist, both of which were very dead.

He held the painting up and tilted it back and forth. Sharp shoulders, sharp elbows, sharp cheeks. For the Bahamut's sake, even her lips were sharp. He grunted. He didn't see how such a birdlike djinn could murder as many people as were rumored. That question alone left him bubbling with curiosity.

He glanced at the squat little matchmaker who had traveled so far to seek him out. The Ahmaran's silk, striped pants were smeared with the red sand of Ghaluma, and his periwinkle skin showed purple blotches of moonburn along the bridge of his nose and under his tired eyes. He stood uncomfortably in the doorway of the warlord's white canvas tent, sweat dripping in wet beads that darkened the sand by his feet everywhere they fell. His own fault for wearing so many layers in a baking desert.

The matchmaker leaned forward, hands clasped. "Well, Chieftain Pardaj, would you like to hear the stipulations of the proposal?"

"What's the Queen of Ahmar want with me?" Pardaj tossed the painting back at the matchmaker who caught it with a fumbling gasp. "The last Ghaluman who dared to suggest a marital union with the purple queen left with his beard split and lashes across his face that spelled her name." He chuckled. "Sheemok has never looked better."

The matchmaker settled his flapping arms with a *harrumph*. He set the portrait down and straightened his tunic. "The Queen of Ahamr requires very specific qualifications. Qualifications, it turns out, you happen to possess."

"Yeah?" Pardaj grunted. "The queen's forefather thought the same of my grandfather Watalam's sister. Plucked her up and didn't give her back. Though she made sure he burned for that, like a true Ghaluman."

"Ah..." The matchmaker twitched, failing to speak several times. "I am sorry for your lost ancestor's circumstance. It is normally a great honor to be considered as a suitor to the throne of Ahmar."

Pardaj scoffed and raised a black brow, trying to find color in the matchmaker's beady eyes. The dim light inside the tent was no help, though they appeared shamelessly clear. The pretentious idiot believed what he was saying.

"Wouldn't I have to be looking to suit to be considered a suitor? Doesn't that make you the one coming to suit me?"

The matchmaker nodded. "We can look at it that way if you'd like."

"I'd like."

The matchmaker cleared his throat and pulled himself up to his full, pathetic height—a torso shorter than Pardaj's own. "May I officially enter your abode?"

Pardaj jutted his jaw up at the sniveling request. "Do as you like, just don't traipse sand across my floor."

The matchmaker's eyes widened, clearly befuddled about what exactly that meant, since all the floors were made of sand.

Pardaj smirked. "Get on with it already, I hate wasting the First Moon's light."

"Very well," the matchmaker said, squirming. He took a few more steps into the shade of the tent, and after scanning the spartan space for a place to sit, decided none were good enough for his spoiled Ahmaran can and stayed standing. "As the entreated party in this proposition of marriage, Qadira, Queen of Ahmar, proposes you become her husband and de facto king of Ahmar for as long as she lives. This union includes a right to a stipend of one hundred thousand dinars a month. You are also required to live in her palace and forsake your land wars in Ghaluma and to promise that you'll help produce an heir immediately. All other stipulations are up for negotiation once a firstborn has been acquired."

"Ah." Pardaj chuckled, running a finger over his brow as all the pieces began to fall into place. "The queen's baby-hungry, and the only seed strong enough to survive the hellfire of her womb must come from the hellish desert of Ghaluma."

"The union can only be seen as a step up for you," the matchmaker continued, ignoring him. "For anyone in this war-torn land. Wouldn't it be nice to wake up every morning at ease that your kingdom and rulership are safe?"

Pardaj barked out a laugh and flexed the muscles under his exposed red skin. "Safe? Is that really the pitch you're going for with the Sparkling Queen? The Slaughterer of Servants. The Eliminator of Innocents. The Maker of Massacre. She makes the warlords of Ghaluma look like little boys play-fighting with sticks."

"Would not marrying her give you the biggest stick?"

Pardaj shrugged, though the man had a point. He hated it when haughty snots had a point. Especially ones from Ahmar.

He ran his tongue over his front teeth and narrowed his eyes. "You just said one of the stipulations is me giving up my land here in Ghaluma. Becoming homeless and living off the nonexistent mercy of a bloodthirsty queen sounds like *marleki* feck to me."

"Not homeless," the matchmaker interjected. "Just re-homed. Ahmar would be where you made your hearth."

Pardaj grunted, turning from the squashy man and crossing to the back of the tent. With a flourished spin, he faced the matchmaker once more and sat with a huff in a pile of worn pillows. "Ahmar is a land of waste. They ship our sand over there, harden it into glass, and then break it back down so it's shimmery and sharp. They bathe in the stuff we wash from between our toes. It's like a bird chewing up worms and spitting them out for its chicks, only the glitter over there isn't used to feed anyone. It's used to suffocate."

"Sand is sand, is it not?" The matchmaker raised a brow.

Pardaj narrowed his eyes.

"I thought a Ghaluman's motto was *home in hearth not place of birth.*"

"It is." Pardaj chewed on his cheek.

The matchmaker's words were just enough to fan the flames of desire and conquest that lived in all Ghaluman's hearts. He was getting old for Ghaluman war standards, having survived far more land skirmishes and minor wars than most. He plumped the pillows behind him, brushing off some sand.

His back did ache, though he'd slit his own throat before he said that aloud, and roaming the sands of Ghaluma day in and day out had long ago lost its appeal. He remained keenly aware that his second-in-command was fomenting a small coup, and all previous wives had perished through childbirth. Maybe now was the time to get out, take some time to relax in luxurious, birdish comfort, and breathe. And if living there became intolerable, with some good rest under his belt, he'd be ready to take over Ahmar and get rid of the purple queen.

"A hundred-thousand dinar, you said?" He confirmed. "That I can do with as I please?"

The matchmaker nodded, the pathetic blue of hope coloring his eyes.

"And she won't murder me in my sleep or anything?" He watched the matchmaker's eyes closely, leaning forward on the pillows. "I've heard a story or two about what she did to her siblings. About how she killed the little one. I'm all for a broad who can hold a sword, but I don't do dirty tricks."

"No tricks." The matchmaker held his open palms out to the side, but the pink of uncertainty glinted in the middle of his irises.

Pardaj grunted.

In the end, it was all the same. The Queen of Ahmar was famous for her temper, silly death sentences, and ridiculous need for sparkly sand. No one trusted her. And if no one could trust the queen, then at least he could trust in that. Either way, if things went gharb, he could always slit her throat first.

CHAPTER TEN

DEE

DEE DID NOT LAND next to her bloodservant as she had planned. Normally, she'd pass through the white between worlds, touch a foot on the barrier for Ard, and push back, landing with a swirl of limey smoke next to whoever she planned on seeing.

This time, she touched Ard, headed toward wherever Vawk may be, and jerked down a tight, black tunnel. If the paths had been tangible, she'd have scraped her elbows and knees, her face and shoulders. But the journey between and within worlds consisted of only fire. Her lime green sparked and hissed, bombarded on all sides by unwelcome firewalls and invasive pokes. Then she tumbled out the other side, her fire steaming through the barrier which created the lime smokiness from her otherwise smokeless djinn fire.

She landed hard on her tailbone and cried out in pain.

Embarrassing.

She growled because the being was right. What was she? Eleven again with her budding breasts, widening hips, and fire coming in for the first time? She hadn't learned how to handle the first two at all, but she had been apparating for two years now and was proficient enough. That was, when she wasn't being stuffed through a fire corridor and puked out the other side... or forgetting where firewalls were set up in the palace like she had that morning.

"Oh, shut up, you horrible creature." She snapped and grabbed the pulsing earring so she could rip it off.

Oh yes, take me off and cast me aside. Let someone else find me. Someone more agreeable who will help me kill you for your insolence. Or you can let me help you kill them first. Them and anyone else who threatens your life during this Allaedam. It's the less painful option, I'm sure you'll agree. Then, you can release me as your first act as my devout queen.

"I am not your devout."

She wanted to crush the earring against the wall, but his threat was real. She couldn't tell if she was using his magic or not. And if that's all it took for him to escape the moment the glass shattered, she was in trouble. She couldn't free him any more than she could risk letting someone else find him.

Her lips quivered. "I'll never release you, nor use your evil magic, you—"

A snap sounded down the hall. Her eyes widened, and fear raced through her with renewed vigor. No servants remained in the palace. Her stalker had arrived.

Dee jumped to her feet and pressed herself to the nearest wall. Her heart pounded in her throat, making it difficult to swallow. She took a quick survey of the empty hallway. White marble with blue veins. She must be near the throne room. She tried to apparate to her rooms, just in case, but the firewall surrounding wherever she had been dumped forbade it.

What had Lahm said? Malqum's lecherous visitors could walk in and apparate out. Perhaps, being allowed to appear wherever they wished after his visits was too much freedom. They must have been re-routed through here. And if Malqum didn't want them seen... Dee tapped her chin, scanning both sides of the hall.

If he was trying to keep secrets and she was near the throne room, this exit corridor probably lay on the sharq side of the palace. That was where the servants entered and exited the throne room during important events and would have allowed decent cover for fleeing courtesans.

Wherever she was, she needed to leave. Whoever had appeared in the room would end up exactly here if—*when* they followed.

Dee glanced back and forth down the dark paths. Then, she darted off at a run and jutted left. Right. Left. And one last right that revealed a crease of light. She darted towards it, desperate to see if she could apparate as soon as she entered the glow. A thick brocade curtain hung at the end, the sliver of light winking at her, mocking and inviting.

She burst through and gasped.

The throne room was nearly unrecognizable, the blue-veined marble hidden under carnage and completely bereft of servants and courtiers. Only the clear dome that showed the stars above remained unchanged. Jagged gashes cut through the floor-length curtains that lined the room. Red streaked the torn pillows of the royal bench where her ma had always sat, cross-legged in her harem pants, to attend to the business of the country. Feathers floated in white tufts, innocent softness in a room hard and full of blood. A purple and lifeless hand, seared with the emblem of a bloodservant, stuck out from behind the platform; a life used as a shield, most likely, unless her master lay dead, too.

The red-painted nails matched that of Dee's sister, Bruella, who always wore her lips in a shade to match.

Dee's gaze darted around the room, looking to see if her sister still lived.

A scream shattered the air to her right. Two of her sisters battled, stumbling out from behind a pillar.

Sixteen-year-old Bruella fought closest to Dee, long black hair studded in emeralds and blood running down her pale-purple cheek and into her lips. She held a dagger in one hand, sweat dripping liberally down her frantic face. Their older, blade-wielding sister, Icha, followed, anger flashing in her stunning green eyes. Her light blue, silk dress was less bloody than Bruella's, her slender neck and toned arms less sweaty as she bested their sister at every turn. It made sense, Icha had been throwing royal gemstone knives for fourteen of her eighteen years of life. No one was better in all of Ahmar. The javelin in her hand and half-dozen royal knives tucked into her belt were a testament to that. Their gem-cast and twisted blades winked in the sconcelight, as horribly expensive as they were deadly.

Bruella blocked a spinning dagger with a *clang* before falling back to the very edge of the throne room. She was running out of room, being boxed into a corner. Her eyes darted to Dee.

Icha didn't wait. An Ahmaran deep-bladed javelin swished past, slicing off a lock of Bruella's hair before the ruby tip impaled itself in an alabaster pillar between them. Another dagger sunk itself into Bruella's bicep. She screamed and stumbled closer to Dee. Dee yelped and drew back, her eyes locking with Bruella's.

They stared at each other, panting, and despite the blood and horror, the act felt strangely familiar. Like when Lahm caught them both when they played hide-and-seek as children and they had to run. Dee's eyes widened. She knew what was coming next.

"Bruella, wait—"

A flash of apology streaked through Bruella's fear-blackened eyes, then, she ran.

"Wait!" Dee cried again, reaching for her.

But Bruella pelted across the floor and slid out into the hallway, then disappeared in a flash of green smoke.

And why are you calling back a sibling who wants to kill you?

"I don't want to be alone with Icha." Dee kept back a hysterical sob, eyes darting around the room, worried a weapon would fly at her from an unseen corner. She had lost sight of Icha. She only hoped her death would be swift.

You could let my magic out. I'd be happy to make it so you aren't alone with Icha. I'd be happy to make it so there is no Icha.

"No." Dee clenched her teeth. "I said no."

Then I suggest you run, trembling mud-tredder.

Dee nodded and made to follow, but Icha flew into her path, eyes murderous and shining with the copper of defiant bravery. She held a curvy emerald dagger that glinted with Bruella's blood. Green and red and utterly terrifying.

"Guess I'm killing you today, instead, sister," she sneered and licked her cut lip.

Dee stumbled backward, feeling frantically along the draperies for the one that held the secret passageway. Her hands pushed against wall after wall. Without success. Icha sprinted closer and closer.

"Icha!" Dee cried, dodging a murderous swipe. "Stop!"

Icha's eyes flashed black and green. "One of us has to die, sister. It will not be me."

"Help," Dee begged uselessly. A figure caught her eye further down the room. Simple dress and a brand on their hand. Icha's bloodservant. What had been his name? "Dondon? Help! Spare me, a sacred heir to the throne."

Icha scoffed and shot a glance at her servant. "You dare elicit *my* bloodservant for help? Your very existence means his death. Besides, the coward has proved himself sniveling and useless in battle. He hides in the curtains instead of doing what needs to be done despite his years of training.." She turned her eyes back to Dee. "Much like you."

"Please!" She looked to Dondon again, but Icha was right. He wouldn't help her. Couldn't. No one could. The Allaedam decreed it so. Only Vawk could assist her because his life depended on hers. But Vawk wasn't there.

There was only her and Icha, the older sister who had barely looked down at Dee her whole life, preparing for the day she would have to kill her. Dee, in turn, had wasted time admiring her sister's pretty hair and graceful walk, too young and naive and stupid to know better.

Lahm had never wasted time on such frivolous things.

Dee hit another wall and dashed sideways as the sapphire blade sliced through the curtain, creating a deep tear that frayed threads and left them ragged.

"Help!"

I can help you, mortal. Call on my magic, and let me aid you.

"Quiet," Dee gasped, reassessing her place in the room.

She shook her head and whimpered. She must have fled too far. There was no way she stumbled into the throne room this far down the wall. She needed to double back. Dee clamped her teeth, a cry in her throat as she tripped down the next set of curtains, dodged another blood-coated blade of her elegant sister, and swung back around.

This Icha needs to die, does she not? Kakkab growled. *Yet, you will not do it. I don't believe you can. Let me help you. I do not fear death as you do. Death is within me and I within it. If you would just—*

"Shut up," Dee hissed, distracted.

Icha thrust forward, a wildness in her normally poised eyes. Her long braid had come undone, framing her face in untamed curls that she got from their mother. Icha had always been the prettiest of them all, but now she looked unhinged. Desperate. And while she had never looked at Dee with love, Icha had also never looked at her with murder. Until then. Icha wiped a dash of blood from her unstained lips and took a slow, deliberate step for every frantic one of Dee's. Nearly upon her, Icha slipped another sapphire dagger from her bag, tossed it gently to readjust her grip, then slashed fast.

"Stop!" Dee begged, pain bursting across her bicep in deep red lines. She wrenched herself away, jumping over a bench that lined the walls of the room and kicking it out toward Icha. Her sister stopped it with her foot and snarled.

Pain and blood wept from Dee's arm. She touched the red and held up her stained fingers, then looked past it at Icha's face.

"You cut me, sister." She rubbed the crimson on her hand and blinked, stupidly surprised her sister had drawn blood.

"*Sister, sister,* that's the problem, isn't it?" Icha snarled. "You had to be my sister and put me through this."

"I put you through this?" Dee shook the shock from her mind.

She needed to get out. To run for her life as Bruella had. Icha blocked the main palace doors, which meant the passage she had come through was her best bet out. With her back firmly against the wall of curtains, she began combing through them in search of her escape.

No exit. No use.

Icha kicked the bench back at her, bruising Dee's shins and pinning her in place against the wall. She yelped and squirmed her way to the edge, the cuts on her eyes stinging and adrenaline coursing through her body telling her that staying alive was the most important thing in all the world.

Dee's limbs still shook from her earlier climb to the fifth-story window. Lahm had been wrong in his timing. Finding King Malqum's room hadn't helped. If anything, all it had managed to do was get him killed and leave her weak, a shadow with nobody to cling to. If he could be wrong, she really stood no chance.

Icha smirked, though her eyes were tired. She pulled a cloth from a hidden pocket and wiped clean her knife, then came in for the kill, swinging down.

Dee shimmied the last bit of the way out from behind the bench and slapped her spine against the next curtain, then fell back through the hidden opening.

She didn't hit the floor. Her body crashed into another, and she fell into a tangled pile of limbs and racing hearts. Dee tried to orient her spinning sight, pulling herself from a thigh clad in Ahmaran's deep, royal purple and cream. The thigh of an heir. She lifted her head and met Hulon's wide eyes.

"You little—" Icha's screech cut off as soon as she ripped the curtain back.

The sconcelight of Eternal Flame that always lit the royal throne room illuminated Hulon's sharp gaze and furrowed brows.

Icha's eyes flashed white as they darted between the two. Her gaze blackened with terror. She ran, but Hulon was faster. He jumped to his feet and sprinted through the curtain, grabbing Icha's wrist as she squealed and begged. The thick brocade fell close, leaving Dee in the dark.

Dee climbed to her feet and leaned against the wall, blood streaming down her arm and onto her hands, red fingerprints on white marble. The bitter and warm smell of djinn fire wept from the shallow slashes on her arm.

You should probably run, Kakkab's deep and ethereal voice slithered once more through her mind.

Dee nodded, gasping as she used the wall for support. Her shins smarted as badly as her shoulder had the time Hulon had knocked her from a tree when she was six. She had thought it an accident at the time, being so young and innocent. So foolish. But Lahm had made sure to tell her that wasn't the case. Her eldest brother, who for anyone but an Ahmaran heir would be a protector, was out for her blood even then. Ma shipped Hulon off to the Vespar fronts shortly after, or Hulon would have already finished the job.

A clanging clattered from the other side of the curtain. Dee shot her head up toward the curtain.

Icha screamed.

Hulon growled, doing things she couldn't even imagine.

Kakkab was right, whatever creature he may be. She should escape while she had the chance. But how could she? She wasn't made for this game. For killing. She couldn't stand by and listen to Icha's desperate begging while Hulon destroyed her. Could she?

Dee took a trembling step toward the curtain.

You're choosing to stay? Kakkab half-sneered, half-growled. *You're ridiculous.*

"I can't do nothing."

And why not? That is the whole purpose of this silly, palace game, is it not?

"It's not a game," she snapped.

And what do you plan to do about it, a sniveling little girl with no skills or courage?

She stopped, doubt creeping in. "Be a distraction? Give her a chance to get away?"

And get yourself killed, no doubt. Kakkab let out a hissing grumble. *If you refuse to spare yourself and run, you should at least go in prepared to finish the handsome man off, first. There's a cunning glow to his eyes. A taste of something muted but powerful. Destroy him first. Then, you can slit the exhausted girl's throat after.*

Needle pricks broke out across Dee's skin. "I don't want to kill."

You plan to enter a battle unwilling to fight. Kakkab's chuckle curdled in her empty stomach. *So you go, like a lamb to the slaughter.*

Lamb.

Lahm.

What had she done? Tears sprung to Dee's tired eyes. Icha's guttural pleas tore through the curtain.

Lahm would tell her the same as the demon in her ear. To take the advantage. That it would be a wasted opportunity. But she couldn't even think of sliding a blade into someone's heart, just like she couldn't shoot the fluffy rams. She grabbed at her chest, wishing she were anywhere but Ahmar. But it was no use and a waste of time. She bit her tongue hard enough to keep her in the present.

She would stick with her rough plan. Unable to kill Icha, she could at the very least help distract Hulon long enough that Icha could do it—end him instead of her. She could make her run for it after that and pray that Icha would be either too grateful or too tired to pursue for at least another day.

If she'd even last another day. Another ten degrees. Another moment. But that was all she needed to try to figure out a plan. A single moment to think, to grieve.

To accept her inevitable death.

Dee swallowed hard, gathering whatever threads of Lahm's courage still lingered within her. Lahm had said she was good and kind, that she was better than the blood expected of Ahmar. If she was going to lose this melee anyway, she might as well be what he thought her to be until she died. Right now, that meant helping Icha. She straightened her shoulders, took a deep breath, and sprinted through the curtain.

CHAPTER ELEVEN

THE GOOSE

THE CELESTIAL CONSTELLATIONS GATHERED once every millennium when a circle of ovals and dots reached a completion and stretched thin into a line. When centuries of moments, decades of weeks had passed and somehow inextricably connected back together again. Circular time in what reassembled a necklace found on a mortal's neck as they lived their fleeting lives, specks of dust in the cosmos.

The Goose had let thousands of these gatherings pass, not caring one wit. What did he have to do with the mess the larger constellations made of the universes? With cosmic clashes and the creation of new planets that would have no intelligible life on them for a dozen string stretches, if at all? And what business was his, the arguments that led to black holes as one Celestial tried to suck power from another?

He'd yawn if he had a mouth. Instead, he found his delights in the intricacies of the tiny and overlooked.

His favorites were the Yitnonny, a strange creation of teeth and fur and slimy eyes that were incredibly profound while fantastically prone to bad tempers. They lived on a shadow planet that circled a baby blue star in the purview of his constellation and were incredibly susceptible to his pulsing magic. But then they had to go and take his words too far and commit genocide. A minor offense when a star is involved, and one Celestials rarely concerned themselves with. The only problem lay in who the Yitnonny ferociously worshiped as their god of gods—an affront to Allah, not that any star seemed to care.

As it turned out, the temples toppled in the series of unfortunate events that led to the planet's destruction belonged to none other than Kakkab, the Celestial of Death.

Which led Anser to attend one of these gatherings of constellations he so ardently attempted to avoid. A summons by the macabre Star of Fatalities to the court of other pretentious big-name constellations so he could condemn the Little Goose of atrocities against the universe and have his death started—sentenced to another billion years before he expanded and burst, flinging precious metals across the universe.

There were worse ways to go, he supposed—like having the lesser stars he ruled ripped from his constellation and given to another before being torn apart by a black hole—but he didn't want to go at all.

"Anser!" Ursa Major's aura verberated with his name, angry and bored at the same time. The salacious supernova.

Anser's aura shivered in the quake of such a monstrous force. "If I may speak—"

"You may not."

Anser bristled. "That hardly seems fair."

"Fairness is of no consequence in the eternities. But what do you know of fairness? Your very words are poison. You use your magic for evil."

"Evil?" Anser coiled his aura tightly around him.

Mischievous misfortune was hardly evil. One ended life, the most sacred gift of all. The other gave mortals who were willing to pay a price the opportunity to take a chance, throw a dart at the heavens, and see if they could avoid death... or not. According to his whims.

The insinuation of evil was revolting. Allah had bestowed magic upon him unasked, the same as all the other stars. Anser hadn't had a say in what kind it was. He had always been taught it was a tool. He simply made sure as many mortals as possible were able to use it, unlike Ursa and Hercules who hoarded their magic for no good reason.

No, he wasn't the bad star here.

Anser bolstered his aura and sent out a shaft of light. "Who dare accuse me of such? Reveal their evidences."

A great trembling shook the stars present in a cosmic tempest, flashes of blue and purple and green and white swirling about between their auras.

"You know the evidence I bring, Goose." The deep voice of Kakkab the Terrible sounded like the crash of two planets colliding.

Anser's core flared out with bursts of heat, but he refused to back down. "The Yitnonny live within my constellation. They are mine to rule."

"Yet you destroyed them out of jealousy."

"Jealousy?" Anser's aura shook with laughter. "Why would I be jealous of you?"

Kakkab's crashing voice warmed with smugness. "Because they worshiped me as a god."

"Some god," Anser snarked. "You couldn't even keep them from their own apocalypse."

"You will suffer!" Kakkab cracked.

Anser puffed out his aura, an impossible snarkiness swelling within him. There was no way Ursa would take his side and risk angering the Demander of Desiccation. He'd be snuffed no matter what he did. So why give in to the hot-cored bully?

He pushed his aura out, light and easy and full of disdain, the Celestial version of the mortal smirk. "Make me."

A cacophonous torrent ripped between them. Kakkab's frightening presence loomed larger and thicker, like freezing smoke and deep-throated cries as he tried to cross through the galaxies and snuff out Anser's closest star.

"Enough!" Ursa Major's mind sliced through them with quiet authority.

The rumbling stopped in an instant, though Kakkab still broiled with bubbling anger. Anser's magic shivered from the assault.

Ursa continued, as sharp and calm as ever. "He will be punished, Kakkab, if for no other reason than forgetting his place among the core Celestials that make up the eternities. But you must not touch him or his little stars. Must not listen to his whispers. So strong is your magic, yet you succumb to his suggestions just like the mortals."

Kakkab's aura cracked and boiled. "If you would let me end him—"

"I won't hear of it," Ursa snipped. "The Goose's voice in your ear has done far more harm than good."

Anser balked. "He has a short temper. You cannot blame that on me."

"Quite, Goose." She cracked, the soft sharpness of her aura permeating every crevice of his. "Return to your place in the heavens, each of you, and the sentence for your misconduct will be decided by the end of the century. Kakkab," she added with a warning, "stay on your side of the galaxies. Even you can lose your way in his tongue. If your aura touches his, who knows what will happen."

Another cracking snap tore through the present auras and ripped them all back to whence they came. But as Anser settled into his home solar system, the little blue planet where once dwelled the Yitnonny spinning peacefully within view, a deep bellow surrounded him, foreign in the silence of space.

A forceful blow the weight of ten stars smashed into his aura.

Kakkab, the Slayer of All, had come to end him.

They tangled and merged, blow for blow. Pure magic radiated out in cataclysmic shock waves that obliterated the planets in his home solar system. If there were any Yitnonny left, there could never be again.

Anser's smaller aura began to crack in half, magic streaming out of him without control or conscience. He was dying, being torn in half faster than a star was ever meant to be, creating rifts in the cosmos. But Kakkab was taking damage, too. Chunks of his aura blasted off into space. Planets wilted in their wake and baby stars trembled, knocked off their course. If they continued much longer, insatiable black holes would form and take life from their universe and give it to another.

He wouldn't make it. Not at this rate. Not with his power streaming uselessly into the black. He had to gain control. Hit for hit, Kakkab would always win. Anser scrunched tight as he sustained another blow. And another. And another. Crack-crack-cracking under the weight of Kakkab's sheer force.

Then a string reached for him through the explosion of intertwined auras, amplified by powerful magic that refused to be ignored. A mortal devout, of which he had so few, beseeched him. Him and Kakkab. Chaos and death. Mischief and the macabre. Kakkab noticed, too, his aura pricking near the edges. It came from Qaf, a tiny nothing planet over fourteen lightyears away.

A call for a daughter. A call for last hope. And it would be, for whoever this mortal was and for Anser, alike.

The Goose thinned his aura out to a string and looped it around Kakkab's rumbling and frigid smoke, then pulsed what remained down in a steady stream toward the mortal.

Kakkab tightened. "What are you doing?"

"What I do best, big brother."

"Release me, dwarf, the cosmos need balance. I must exist. Life without death is unsustainable. Worlds will crumble. Your very—"

Anser looped around Kakkab once more and squeezed, pulling them both through the plea that still hooked into his center, and they disappeared from the heavens.

CHAPTER TWELVE

Dee

Dee burst through the curtain and back into the throne room before she could lose her courage. She scanned the empty and spacious rooms. The dim and swirling lights of the cosmos shone through the glass dome overhead, orbs of color that danced across the floor to a silent Celestial song.

Icha and Hulon hadn't gone far, fighting near the raised platform that hid Bruella's dead servant. Dee fell back, slipping on blood that now streaked the marble floor.

Hulon swung his scimitar hard in a flash of emerald. Icha barely blocked, but his blade slid down her own, threatening her fingers. She pulled back, and he knocked her dagger from her hand. He knocked Icha to her knees and held her by the hair, her chin tilted back with his blade at her throat.

Dee gasped and, desperate, yanked Icha's javelin from the nearby column. She ran forward and gave it a clumsy throw. It clattered to the ground at his feet. He looked up, surprise flashing in his deep green eyes. Icha didn't waste the opportunity, headbutting Hulon who yelled in anger and scrambled away.

Icha dove for the main hallway, but Dee knew better than to let her cross the apparation barrier. She needed to keep Icha there to fight Hulon. To finish him before he could wield his scimitar in Dee's direction. At least, that's what Lahm would say.

Dee darted in front of her, realizing only then that she had no weapon. Nothing but outstretched arms kept her siblings at bay. Luckily, Icha was tired, blood-soaked, and panting. She came to a halt between where Dee stood and where Hulon had risen to his feet.

Icha snarled like a caged animal.

Hulon smirked and shifted back into a deceptively relaxed pose. "I thought Lahm's fall an accident, if I am honest, little Qadira," he said, his voice smooth as liar's milk. "Now, I wonder."

Dee's chest rose and fell in heavy bursts.

Are you not going to answer? The exchange of clever banter is the fun part of fighting with someone you know.

"Shut up," she hissed.

Hulon's eyebrows rose. "Meek little *Dee Dee Ra* is telling me to shut up?"

"I—"

Leave it, Kakkab hissed with a laugh. *Let him think you suddenly brave.*

She hardened her face, unable to deny the cunning wisdom that floated from her earring.

Between them, Icha trembled, sliding so her knees bumped together. "Sister." She glanced first at Dee, then looked to Hulon. "Brother." Her voice shook as she stuck out her chin. "Let us either lay down our arms or finish this."

I like her.

"Enough."

Hulon's smirk grew as he flipped a ruby dagger back and forth in his hand. "Shall we let little Qadira decide? Can a shadow act on its own?"

The snickers in her ear grew, heating her blood. But what could she say? Hulon was referring to Lahm, the better half of their twinship. Everyone felt the same. That he was born first and was better in every way, that she was a shadow that sucked away his full potential.

She had spent her life trying to be just that—a shadow with hands that moved on its own, working to aid Lahm in whatever he did. Because whenever she tried to act without him, she failed.

And now she was exactly as Hulon described. A shadow without a person. A wandering ghost, except she lived when Lahm didn't. Could a ghost have a shadow?

Could it have two?

Icha wiped the blood from her lip and adjusted the grip on her sapphire blade. "I decide my fate."

She sprinted toward Hulon, their blades colliding in swift arcs of blue and red. Sapphire and ruby and hints of blood, backlit by the light and dark greens of their fire raging and pouring from hands and eyes.

Dee drew back, fully realizing her terrible mistake.

You really are useless, then, hm?

"I—I—" she stuttered, shame creeping into her lavender cheeks.

You don't know who you are or what you want. So why try to live at all? Jump between their blades and finish yourself so we no longer have to look at you.

"I may not know what I *do* want, but I know what I don't want. To murder and kill."

So you want to die.

"That is not what I said."

But that is the choice you're making. If you don't want to kill, then you will be killed. It has been that way since you were born.

"It is unjust," she spluttered, eyes filling with hot tears that blurred the fight before her. "To me and all my siblings."

Life is unjust. To the pauper who fights daily to live for want of food. And the sick who fight daily against an illness not their own. To the mother screaming in childbirth, giving her life so another can live. To the farmer whose crops die because the sky refuses to rain. To the abandoned child created and discarded before they've had a chance to live. Don't waste tears crying over injustice, princess. You will ne'er find a sympathetic ear. Everyone is far too obsessed with their own injustices to care for yours.

"Lahm cared," she whispered.

And then you killed him.

Rage-filled tears flooded her cheeks. "I will kill you next then, shall I?"

Silence.

"I *will* kill you next!"

She raised her fist, now clutching a glittering blade made of deep-set onyx, a stone said to dampen djinn fire and shatter in a person's heart. She had no idea where it came from or how she came to hold it, but she knew what it was for.

A scream pulled her eyes from the dagger. A deep cut tore down the middle of Icha's dress, thick blood obscuring her sister's purple breasts. Hulon, too, sported a fair share of knicks, sticky red dripping into his shining eye from a split brow. They were a formidable match. A general and a markswoman. Both far more prepared and deadly than Dee.

Icha stumbled away from him, colliding with Dee before she could run. Dee shouldered the weight, knowing if she was knocked down, Hulon wouldn't give her a chance to stand back up. Her feet slipped in the flowing blood, warm and sticky between her toes. The smell made her gag, but she pushed Icha off her, gripping the newfound blade in her hand. Just in time.

Hulon thrust himself towards them, scimitar raised. He slashed down between the two as Dee shoved Icha away. Cold wind whipped past her face, and Hulon stumbled, revealing his chest in a perfect opening.

The black dagger hummed in Dee's hand. Snickers in her ear.

Let me do it.

She resisted, pulling the dagger to her chest though it yearned to plunge into that of her greater foe's. She could no more push the blade into death than she could the devilish earring.

But Hulon did not share such qualms. He caught Icha in his stumble and spun her around so her back faced Dee. He glanced at her, keen eyes saying everything and nothing at all. Then, he smirked and shoved Icha toward her.

The onyx blade slid easily into her sister's back, slurping as it went. Dee felt the squish of muscle and viscera in her very veins. Icha screamed, guttural and gurgling as blood filled up her lungs. Bile seared Dee's throat. Horror, her heart.

Dee let go, hands shaking too hard to hold the knife. Icha fell forward, gagging and coughing up blood. Then a clatter from the far side of the room as Dondon, too, fell in a writhing mess and choked on blood that was not his own, his honored fate as bloodservant. Black fear filled Icha's eyes black, dark as the Moonless Night. Then her wrist flicked one last time, and an amethyst dagger the color of Dee's skin sunk high into Hulon's chest.

Hulon stepped back, white shock flashing in his eyes. He dropped his arm, so the tip of his scimitar hit the ground, then ripped the dagger from just below his clavicle. "That little—" he rasped. Then threw the knife on Icha's dying body before turning to Dee. "It seems you are *my* shadow now, sister. Do a better job and kill the next one off faster, hm?"

"You did this," Dee stammered, "not I." She wanted to help Icha as she coughed out her and Dondon's life but knew Hulon would end her the moment she did.

Icha's death had to be. Hers and Lahm's and five others.

"It is your blade and her blood that tell the true story." Hulon tilted his head, a namur watching prey twitch under its paw. "And what a blade it is. Such strong magic, I could feel it as it sucked away her life. I underestimated how far Lahm got in preparing you for this day. Or perhaps I underestimated you this whole time, for you stand before me and he's nowhere to be found. It was smart, killing your mentor off first. Unexpected, for sure, but that's what made it so delicious for you, isn't it?"

The words he spewed made her stomach knot. She wanted to curl up in bed and die slowly of a broken heart, but even that would be murder, wouldn't it? Since poor Vawk only lived if she did.

As much as she hated the belligerent being that now whispered in her ear, she couldn't deny the heavy weight in his ever-flowing words.

That's right, Kakkab's ephemeral voice sifted through her. *Djinn will die no matter what you choose, death-bringer. So you might as well live.*

Hulon pressed his palm over the wound in his chest with a grimace. "Now if you'll excuse me, I have a wound to attend to."

He turned to leave, and Dee scrambled for the dagger he had tossed on Icha's body. But as she approached, the blood was too much. She couldn't rob her sister as she lay dying.

"*Huraasi!*" Hulon cried, hunching his shoulders and pulling his collar up to cover his wound and another weeping gash. "Confirm the kill! Another death by the Eighth Heir!"

"Wait," she called after him. "Why are you doing this?"

He glanced over his shoulder at her, cunning in his eyes. "Just follow, dear shadow, and you shall see."

He fled through the stream of guards pouring in, and she growled.

The soldiers lined all the main hallways, observing the fights between siblings but nothing more. They were under strict orders not to kill, to aid, or to intercede, on penalty of death and eternal damnation. All they could do was wait. Wait and see and blow the horns so the entire city could keep up with the games. She clenched her teeth and sticky fingers.

A tall guard approached, his skin a shade of purple so light, his blood must be mixed with Vespar. He clapped his hands together in front of her with a bow, armor jangling, and a giant grin on his face. "Two kills under your belt, Royal Murderess. And what a surprise. Not for me, though. You're keeping my coffers full." He winked, then added, "Long live the Eighth Heir. There can only be one queen."

Her stomach dropped, bile coating her tongue. They were making bets, the lot of them, even as they dragged the dead children of Ahmar from their pools of blood. For this was all a game, wasn't it? To her siblings and Kakkab and the rest of the kingdom. What was it to her? Not that...

Even so, she was winning. Two kills to the Eighth Heir of the throne of Ahmar.

She ran from the room, feet slipping on the blood-stained marble.

You heard the djinn, Kakkab's whisper was back. *There can only be one queen.*

SECOND CULLING

A Formal Allaedam Declaration

By the grace and providence of the Celestial Bahamut on the thirty-fifth day of the Seventh Moon's One-Thousandth Shadow Pass, in the time of the Fifteenth Allaedam to secure the throne of Ahmar, a culling eliminated the weak and chaotic. During the Allaedam, the Eighth Heir of the True Nine who have claim to the throne of Ahmar killed the Sixth Heir by puncture of the heart with an onyx blade of unknown origin in the throne room of the Crystal Palace.

The official record of True Heirs to the Ahmaran throne reads as:

First True Heir, Shutor - Honorably killed by the Third Heir for his country

Second True Heir, Talcum - Honorably killed by the Third Heir for his country

Third True Heir, Hulon - Living at 25 years old

Fourth True Heir, Nazdael - Living at 21 years old

Fifth True Heir, Bruella - Living at 18 years old

Sixth True Heir, Icha - Honorably killed by the Eighth Heir for her country

Seventh True Heir, Lahmdan - Honorably killed by the Eighth Heir for her country

Eighth True Heir, Qadira - Living at 13 years old

Ninth and final True Heir, Chiba - Living at 5 years old

No other deaths are yet recorded as the country awaits the victor of the Allaedam, but with the Bahamut as Ahmar's witness, only one heir can rule.

CHAPTER THIRTEEN

The Meeting

Pardaj marched through the ridiculously opulent palace in the heart of the City of Pearls. Everything shined with a luster that he'd only seen on butter. It smelled similar, too, super fatty and far too greasy. Nowhere in Ahmar was this shiny. It couldn't be with all the sand blowing about. He looked behind him and smirked at the trail of red footprints already being scrubbed from the tile by soft-bellied servants.

He would tear this place apart and return it to sand.

The queen's pompous little servant waddled in front of him, half his size and twice as round. He had to take three steps for Pardaj's every one.

Pardaj rolled his bare shoulders back—as a Chieftan, he never wore a shirt or kaftan— and stretched the leather of his armor so it creaked. "How much farther before we see the ol' braud, Vawky?"

The servant bristled. "Speak of her Magnificence like that again, and your head will roll."

"Maybe," he chuckled. "But then who will sire your silly queen's bony offspring?"

Vawk whirled around and shoved a thick finger into Pardaj's gut—a fly on a riding lizard's spine.

"Listen here, you Ghalumam piece of drakonte scat—"

"Woah, woah," Pardaj laughed. "I think you know better than to insult a Ghaluman."

"Like you could do anything to her Glisterful Gorgeousness." Vawk scoffed. "You've been de-weaponed. You're in a palace surrounded by guards with nothing but your fingernails to do any harm."

"I've done plenty of damage with my fingernails," he said, smiling far too politely as Vawk squirmed.

Of course, he had more than that—a Ghaluman glass blade hidden behind his belt that he wasn't about to give up. He forged it himself with his Gift of Elm from the sands of his homeland. It was the only way to imbue glass with magical abilities and to make it as hard as human steel. Most Ghaluman weapons were made from the stuff, which was part of the reason warlords could only come from the ancient lines of the First Magnate. Without a properly-gened ruler, there would be no weapons.

But as much as he loved the heat-blistered sands of Ghaluma, home was hearth, not place of birth. That presumptuous matchmaker had been right. If he got his way, he'd be making a hearth right in the heart of the City of Pearls. Then, when he got bored enough, he'd set it ablaze and turn the glitter back into sand.

Vawk spluttered complaints about Pardaj's lack of decorum as he led him down corridor after corridor, the gemstones encrusting the marble columns shifting from emeralds to sapphires to rubies to topaz. At last, they reached a towering set of doors that pushed open into a room covered in blue-veined marble. Unlike most of the rulers in Qaf who opted for pillowed comfort and the subtle richness of tapestries and rugs, the queen of Ahmar sat on a high-backed throne made of glistening clear crystal in the middle of the room. Her crown shone like a star, seeming to conjure its own light from within. And on each of the six points glistened a dazzling diamond, one taller than all the rest.

Pardaj straightened his back and squared his shoulders. He had a sudden and pestering need to appear imposing in the face of such luster, however excessive it was. The woman's bright shade of lipstick, alone, made it hard to look at her. The jewels in her crown and her glittering skin only added to the nightmare.

"Your Royal—"

"Astonishingness," the queen cut him off.

He stopped several paces back from her throne and crossed his arms with a smirk. "I was going to say Glibness."

"Guards," the queen shrieked, her voice like nails on glass. She thrust herself from her throne so her crown of crystals wobbled.

Soldiers advanced from their positions along the wall. Pardaj grabbed Vawk by his shiny bald head and lifted him from the ground.

"Come at me, and Vawky here dies."

She flicked her wrist, wrath smoldering in her bright purple cheeks. The guards stopped in their tracks.

Anger flashed green from her eyes. "You dare insult me in my palace?"

Vawk thrashed, grabbing Pardaj's wrists to try and break free like it would do anything.

Pardaj smirked. "You dare kill the djinn you called to seed you? At least, let me bed you like a Ghaluman, first."

"You have angered me." Her bright red lips curled. "Now someone must die."

Pardaj raised his chin. "It ain't going to be me, Glitz."

He expected another torrent of shiny nonsense. Instead, the anger drained from the queen's eyes, which settled into a calm, lizard green. She approached, silk robes trailing behind her in a trail of glitter. She reached him and leaned in close. A strong hint of a million different floral scents—or one powerful one he wasn't familiar with—wafted from her slender neck.

"You do not fear me?"

"A no-nonsense braud with a bad temper?" He chuckled dryly. "Have you been to Ghaluma?"

"Fine." She sneered, her too-red lips slack and condescending. A bemusing mix of yellow disdain and crimson lust played together in her eyes. He often got that reaction from women. "You may bed me. Drop Vawk so he can call in the imams and ready the bedchambers. I wish to get this done as soon as possible."

Pardaj raised his brows, both insulted and fascinated at the queen's presumptuousness. "Hold on a degree. I didn't agree to anything yet."

The glint returned to her eyes, but they stayed clear without a hint of pink. He had to give her one for that. It was the most attractive she had ever looked, bony hips and birdish lips notwithstanding.

"You dare to refuse me?" she asked, her voice dangerous and low.

"I don't offer my seed to any woman whose womb can't hold it. Do you see these shoulders?" He angled toward her and flexed. "Now that I've seen you in person, I've decided you'd never survive. You'd just *pop*, like a ram's bladder filled with too much air."

Green anger flared in her eyes. She stepped back and slashed at his chest with a dagger he hadn't realized she was holding. An amateur move on his part, but he refused to concede any ground as a deep cut tore across his bare pectorals, sizzling from the metal she dared wield against him.

His chest burned painfully in tattered fizzles. He tightened his jaw against the ache and took a slow breath. "Wrong choice, princess."

He snatched his glass blade with his free hand, the other still holding Vawk, and set his foot back, preparing for an attack. Guards streamed from off the wall. The first charged at him with a diamond scimitar. Pardaj ducked, catching the guard on his shoulder so he could throw him over. Vawk dangled with a whimper in his other hand. He spun around and shoved Vawk on top of the guard, then slit the man's throat so the blood splattered across Vawk's face, making his skin look almost Ghaluman. The guard's toes stopped twitching, and Pardaj stood, refusing to wipe the blood off as he turned and faced the horrified queen.

He smiled and picked Vawk back up, then held the soaked blade to his throat.

"Stop!" she screeched.

Every muscle in the room froze before the soldiers skittered back against the wall. Qadira stepped on the dead djinn as she made her way closer, her silk soaking up the blood.

"Problem, 'Dir?" he asked.

And there it was in the very center of her eye. Fleeting pink. He had gotten to her. He smirked.

"Get out," she hissed.

"As you wish." He offered her a deep bow and threw sputtering Vawk at her feet. When he rose, he winked, then turned and left the palace.

Maybe the Glittering Queen wasn't so bad, in a sharp, unpleasant sort of way. If nothing else, she'd be fun to play with. And he was determined he would. It didn't matter how she felt about him, he was going to make his hearth in this palace and return the sand that adorned everything in this place back to Ghaluma.

He just needed to wait for the right moment, and this wasn't it. Only Ahmaran-blooded rulers remained on the throne when a spouse died. If Qadira passed, he would be kicked right back to Ghaluma, landless and at rock bottom, and that's exactly what she'd be if she tried to birth a Ghaluman baby. No, this required thinking. Fortunately, the queen seemed desperate. He'd just wait for her to approach again—he was sure she would—and take the opportunity as it came.

CHAPTER FOURTEEN

Dee

Dee didn't stop to count the bloody footprints that smattered the tile behind her. It didn't matter how many there were, only where they were headed. Which was Jahannam. She had murdered. Twice. Mischief or not, birthright or not, it didn't matter, not to her. Her blade had pierced her sister's heart, and there was no way she could clean the murder off her skin, much less her soul. Her guilt would torment her forever.

The moment her foot touched the hallway, she apparated to her rooms. She'd leave the palace if she could, just apparate to the field where her baba used to take her and her siblings to hunt and disappear from there. But it was forbidden. Once the Allaedam was called, the palace locked down, firewalls keeping all the royals bound until only one of them emerged, victorious and broken. They had learned to hunt in the wild, but now the wild was her home.

I don't see why you're so upset, Kakkab sneered as she traveled toward Vawk in the nothing between worlds. *Do all footed creatures cry so much? It's quite unsettling. Water's a valuable resource in the cosmos, you know. You shouldn't waste it on your pathetic tears.*

She landed on the plush rugs next to her changing rooms and grabbed the earring, ready to rip it from her lobe.

"Qadira!" Vawk rushed forward from the window, hands wringing and face crinkled with inevitable worry. "You live!" He grabbed her hands in his and squeezed, searching her body and *tsking* with every dab of blood he found.

"Of course, I live." She collapsed to her knees, relieved to be around someone who wasn't trying to kill her. Her sticky hands left bloody fingerprints on the cream-colored rug. "You're alive, aren't you?"

Vawk scuttled to the washroom and back with several muslin towels and began scrubbing away at the scarlet of her skin.

"True, too true. But I don't know the state you're in. I experience the same death you do, but until then I don't feel your cuts or your wounds. I don't feel your fear. I simply know your heart is beating because mine is. If you think that does anything for my nerves, I'll tell you now, it doesn't."

A bloodservant, Kakkab mused. *The lengths you djinn go to for loyalty are hysterical.*

She yanked her face out of his hands, her cheeks stinging from his attention and the demon's mockery. "I'm sorry, Vawk. I got here as quickly as I could. Lahm fell, and then Hulon was on my heels. Then Icha—" Her voice broke. "She's dead, on my knife. I didn't kill her. But I also did." She dropped her face into her hands. "Just like Lahm. What am I going to do?"

Vawk pursed his thick lips. "Survive."

"Must I?"

Vawk twitched. "I am understandably supportive of the idea."

She sighed. "I'm sorry, Vawk. I know you want to live, and I'm sorry you're tied to the weakest of all the heirs. It is unfair, but I recently learned that everything is."

"Hm." Vawk leaned in close, his bulbous nose nearly touching hers as he looked at her, a surprising amount of clarity in his naturally black eyes.

"What?" She pulled back, balking at the unspoken interrogation.

"You're not talking like you."

"And why should I?" She bristled. "I've nearly been killed several times today and helped kill two of my siblings. I've also had my oldest living brother betray me by declaring me the murderer so that I'm even more of a target for everyone else. He called me a shadow who is destined to die. I am not who I was this morning so why should I sound like I am?"

"Because you still have things to do," he harrumphed. "Who's left? According to the bonehorns, you have Hulon, who you've miraculously managed to survive."

She winced at his incredulity.

He tapped his chin. "Then there's the witch, Nazdael." He shivered. "She's always hiding in the gloom of the palace, the little bells creeping everyone out. She will be difficult to even find, much less kill."

Qadira's stomach soured. "I don't want to kill anyone, Vawk. It makes me sick."

He tsked her again, walked to a basket on the side table by her door, and grabbed a loaf of bread placed there from breakfast. He walked over, mind anywhere but on what she wanted, and shoved the loaf into her mouth. It tasted of ash, but it gave something for her worrying tongue to do, so she took a bite, then another.

"There's also Bruella," Vawk sighed. "But she shouldn't be too hard. Her head has always been wrapped up in politics and deals, not fighting. Which just leaves—"

A whimper broke the silence in the corner of her room. Dee swung around, her heart in her throat. Vawk stepped between her and the curtain, pulling a curved kilij from his robes that she hadn't once seen him carry a day in his life. Its blade was rare metal that would burn any djinn's flesh, its hilt carefully wrapped wood.

He might as well be a child for how well he wields that blade, Kakkab snickered.

Dee winced and took a step away. "Since when do you carry an Ardish kilij?" she whispered, eyes frantically scanning the pillows across the room.

Does he even know how to use the thing?

Vawk straightened his shoulders without looking back at her. "A guard gave it to me and taught me how to use it this morning."

So, no.

"Vawk..." she started, not sure which was more threatening, whatever hid in the corner or her clumsy bloodservant with a flesh-burning blade.

"Do *you* want to stand between me and the sound in the corner?" He turned and glared at her with a curled lip.

She pouted. "I'm just saying, we did a terrible job preparing for today. Hulon, Lahm, even Icha. They knew what was coming. What was I doing? Seeing if I could drink tea better. Oh, I'm not made for any of this." She threw up her hands and stormed toward the pillows. "You can kill me now, whoever is there. I won't fight you. Just be swift!"

Kakkab laughed, an itching tickle in her ear.

"Qadira!" Vawk snapped.

She threw herself on her knees in front of the pillows, ready to be done with everything and take her penance for what she did. She was nothing without Lahm anyway. A shadow to be struck down so she couldn't be used further by Hulon.

The pillows ruffled, and Vawk scurried in front of her, blocking her view, his hands noticeably sweating on the wrapped handle of his canary yellow scimitar.

"You!" he gasped.

Dee peeked around his plushy side, her pulse thrumming in her palms. Relief broke in sweat down her neck. At best, her declaration had been a hasty bluff she had wanted to believe.

"Chiba?"

The little round face of her five-year-old sister poked from the cushions, tear-streaked and sniffling. "Please, don't kill me, DeeDee."

Dee's heart broke, and she rushed forward to scoop Chiba from the pillow.

Two steps away, a sharpness met her throat, jittering and unsteady.

Dee froze.

"Touch her, and I'll use my dying breath to end you," Chiba's bloodservant declared, her voice as uncertain as her grip on the weapon.

End her. The little djinn isn't worth your chance to live.

Dee raised her hands slowly, ignoring the sting of his words in her ear. "I mean no ill will. Who could harm a crying child?"

"Who could kill their twin brother?" the bloodservant spat.

Dee flinched, the barb sinking directly into her raw heart.

Vawk advanced, the curved end of his kilij directly in front and shaking far too much for comfort. "You know the rules, Sadie. We are not allowed to harm the children of the throne."

"Or what?" Sadie let out a cold laugh, her simple headscarf shaking and her branded hand squeezing the weapon so tightly, it was turning white. "They'll kill me? We're already slated for such death, are we not?"

"And what of the afterlife?" Vawk took another step, so he stood beside Dee, his eyes glancing nervously between her and Chiba's angry bloodservant. "Are you ready to consign yourself to a life of penance for breaking your sacred oath?"

"If Chiba becomes queen, I'll have plenty of time for penance in this life." Sadie glanced unapologetically at Dee, but the weapon at her throat didn't move.

What now, Qa-di-ra? Kakkab interjected, sounding both energized and bored. *She gets it. Your mealy servant even understands. Let me do what I do best.*

"No, you—" Dee snapped far too loudly. She swallowed hard, reminding her of the cold weapon still threatening her neck. She tried to temper her feelings and breathe. "Maybe Chiba and I don't have to die any more than we have to become queen. Maybe we could find a way out of the palace. Maybe we could find a way to fake our deaths. Maybe... Maybe we can escape from this fate pushed upon us."

The pressure on her neck increased before pulling away. Dee slapped a hand around her chaffed skin and glanced warily at what she now could see was a light-green corundum shiv. An effective weapon made from the leg of one of the palace chairs.

She had to smile then. Sadie was braver than Vawk but just as unprepared. And why shouldn't she be? The queen was supposed to live for another hundred years. The melee between royal siblings rarely took place between children.

Children...

Dee glanced at Chiba. Her little sister's simple dress was clean except for a bit of spilled hummus she must have eaten for breakfast, not knowing what that day would bring. Her light-purple cheeks were now raisin-purple and stained with tears. It was her eyes though, that tore at Dee because they matched her own. It was like looking at herself. Like all her worries and fears were wrapped in an adorable and scared five-year-old's body.

Dee knelt and held open her arms. Her little sister burst from the pillows and jumped in as Dee wrapped her up in a tight embrace.

"I'm so scared," Chiba whimpered and buried her face in Dee's shoulder.

"*Takun ealaa alsalam*, Chiba," Dee crooned, then turned to Sadie. "Why are you in my chambers?"

Sadie released a heavy sigh. "Chiba insisted."

Dee scrunched her nose. "Why?"

"Because you and Lahm are the only siblings she knows, having shared the nursery with her until your fire came in. She remembers only you. She knows only you aside from her mama, the queen. Your siblings never bothered to come to visit. She doesn't even have a father to call her own since he passed away shortly after she was born. And for this reason, she believes you, the only family she knows, will protect her."

Precious. Precious and stupid.

The ice in Sadie's eyes stabbed at Dee once more.

"I could only believe she was right and trust that the meek and sweet Qadira I remember was not the same one that pushed her brother out a window. I would draw my own conclusions as to Lahm's death if I could, but I saw no body, only heard the announcement blared out on bonehorns and whispered of throughout the palace."

Vawk lowered his blade, sweat breaking across his forehead. "Gossips."

"What else do they say?" Dee winced as she asked, pulling Chiba closer so her chubby cheek squished against her own, both curious and terrified to hear the answer.

Sadie tilted her chin up, eyeing them both. "That you had been playing with Lahmdan not ten degrees before his death."

Dee pressed her lips tight.

"That you looked down upon his crumpled body from a lofty tower and then turned away, heart cold to what you had done."

You really are a monster, Kakkab cackled gleefully. *Your reputation is as bad as mine, and you've done nothing. You are a murderess by simply being a clutz.*

Chiba sniffed and took Dee's cheeks in her little hands, looking into her eyes. "I told her it wasn't true. You love Lahm. Lahm loves you. And you both love me. I remember."

The contrast between the bodiless voice of death and sweet Chiba broke like waves against Dee's chest, reminding her of who she was. Who they all were. She fought to keep back heaving sobs.

"I'll keep you safe, Chibi Chiba, I promise."

Sadie scoffed, but a pounding on the door cut her short.

Chiba stiffened in her arms, and Dee's eyes shot wide. "You two need to hide."

"Shouldn't we all?" Vawk squeaked, his scimitar now scraping the rug as he paced back and forth, terror clear on his face.

If you disappear, they'll never stop looking.

Dee shook her head, hating that Kakkab was right. It wouldn't take long to strip the room down to bare tacks. And then she and Chiba would both be killed.

"It's possible whoever is trying to get in heard voices. If we all hide, then they'll look. They are probably only expecting you and me, Vawk. If Chiba hides, they shouldn't think to look for her at all."

Vawk's shoulders slumped.

Dee nodded, grateful he was willing to obey.

Hide her. Hide her. Where to hide her?

Her lips curled at the taunt as her eyes swept the room for anything that could work. She spied the thick trunk in front of her bed where she kept her winter blankets.

An interesting choice.

"You wouldn't use it?" she asked in a mutter.

Me? Kakkab went silent as if in thought. *I would find great use for it.*

Dee frowned. "Then why did you say interesting?"

Because I've been locked in a burned bedchamber for two centuries. Everything is mildly interesting now. It's quite a sad state, I will admit.

Dee hesitated. But the pounding on the doors intensified, a hammering meant to tear them off their hinges.

"There," she finally declared, rushing over and creaking open the polished wood top of the trunk.

Dee rearranged the blankets, shoving them down so sweet Chiba could just fit inside.

"Are you sure about this?" Sadie asked, fidgeting. "She should hide somewhere I can hold her. She doesn't like being alone."

Chiba's eyes widened. "I don't want to be alone. It's so dark in there. Monsters hide in the dark. I want Sadie with me. Or you, Dee. Don't leave me. Please, don't leave me alone."

"There's no time." Dee shook her head. "It won't be for long. I promise."

"I trust you." Chiba nodded, warm tears flooding her bright purple cheeks, mirrored green eyes completely black. Her chin wobbled and she wrapped her arms tightly around herself.

Dee looked away as she gently closed the lid, knowing just how she felt about monsters in the dark.

"I trust you," came Chiba's final muffled sniffle.

Dee clenched her jaw and turned to face the room.

"And me?" Sadie asked, voice edgy and shiv twitching in her hands. "I want to be close."

Dee bit her lip, the doors visibly shaking as the assault on them reached thundering. She then pointed to the thick curtains that lined the back of her bed. "You'll have to balance on the banister and hold very still." She pushed Sadie towards them. "But if you stand in one of the folds, you won't be noticed at all."

Sadie nodded, crawling over the silk sheets and disappearing behind the curtain just as the door burst open and Bruella entered, a mace dipped in gold shaking in her hands.

CHAPTER FIFTEEN

THE CHAMBERMAID

HER MOTHER HAD TOLD her not to stray while in the Queen's chambers. She wasn't supposed to be there at all. But her ba was sick with the *famels*, just like half the kingdom every decade or so, and she couldn't be left on her own.

Of course, being six, she hadn't listened to one wit. How could she when everything in the queen's chamber glittered or sparkled or glowed? She wanted to touch it all.

So she did.

While her mother made the bed and fluffed the pillows, she dawned a veil that glistened like the stars. While her mother emptied the chamberpot, she tried on some bright red lipstick that was sticky and wet. And when her mother left to take the dirty linens down the hall to the washmaids, after biting her lip as she decided whether or not to leave her daughter behind, the little girl opened the lid of a large trunk to see what might shine inside.

That's when the doors opened with a ferocious bang, and the little girl toppled inside. She landed in musty blankets, and the lid snapped down over her. Her heart hammered and her pulse raised. The dark was where monsters lived, and she needed to get out. But her umi had said the queen was a monster, too. So instead of screaming, she mustered all the big-girl courage she could and slowly lifted the lid to watch.

The queen marched into the room, black thawb trailing behind her and catching the wind on each turn. She was wonderful, every inch of her shining and sparkly, like a star fallen from heaven. She pulled the open ends of the robe closer together and huffed, stopping in front of a tall mirror.

With narrowed eyes, the queen turned her jaw one way and then the next, angling towards the far corner of the room with each pass. The chambermaid's daughter followed suit, pretending she was looking at herself in the mirror, glittering and beautiful. The queen sucked her cheeks in and puckered, then released with a *smack*. The chambermaid's daughter did the same, eyes widening when her lips *popped* too loud. She cowered down, but the queen didn't notice.

"Acceptable," the queen said at last, though the little girl thought she looked positively divine. "Perfectly acceptable." She smiled and tucked the ends of the thawb closer. "I—"

Her eyes narrowed. She leaned in. The scowl deepened.

"I am not getting old."

She whipped her face to one side and combed hair and a dangling earring back from her jawline, stretching the skin over and over as if smoothing out a silk sheet.

The little girl looked to the side, too, curious who she spoke to, but no one was there.

"I am only fifty-four, you glittering nag," the queen continued. "Not yet a quarter of the way through my life."

A shiver ran through the queen's frame, and she leaned forward until her nose almost touched the mirror. The six largest jewels on her crown tinkled against the glass. She glanced up. Twitched. Then pulled back and huffed.

"This is that wretched healer's fault. Forcing that potion down my throat without warning me at all. Terrors and visions. Remembering forward and forgetting back." The queen paced the floor, whipping her robe at the end each time. "Nightmares..." She paused mid-step and glanced at the large trunk on the far side of the room.

The little girl sucked in her breath and dropped the lid as softly as she could manage.

"Noises coming from the dark," the queen's muffled voice said.

Footsteps carried closer. The sound of fingers brushing against the smooth wood. Then footsteps again, fading.

"Nobody asked for your opinion," the queen's voice was once again distant. "You just give it, whether it's wanted or not."

The air in the trunk felt heavy and tight and made the girl's chest heave uncomfortably. It was enough for her to open the lid for a bit of fresh air.

The queen stood on the far side, once more staring at the mirror. A smile curled on her lips, and she marched forward, chin high.

"That's right, you opulent bit of buklak breath. Not a soul listens to you. Do you think I hadn't noticed? All your threats and promises telling me you can make anything happen were falsehoods. Lies!" She raked her painted nails across the glass in a screechy smear, every crystal on her crown and ears shaking and shimmering.

Her fingers slid smoothly off, leaving only silence.

"Because if you could do anything, you could create life. But no—" She sniffed and turned her back to the mirror. "All you bring is death. And that…"

She shook her head, each sweep of her eyes landing on the dark wooden chest, shorter and shorter until her gaze lingered only there. The girl held her breath, lowering the lid with each sweep, so only a little crack illuminated the inside.

"That…."

The queen turned and took a step closer to the trunk. Then another, one after another until her figure shadowed the carved trunk. She was too close now for the chambermaid's daughter to move at all, and besides, the little girl was afraid of the voices in the dark. The ones the queen had mentioned. So she continued holding her breath as the air around her grew hotter and heavier, only the tiniest sliver of light keeping the darkness at bay.

The queen stood and bent lower, eyes locked on the trunk.

The little girl stared and was sure she saw glistening eyes staring back at her.

The queen's eyes widened. Her fingers curled.

"You did this," she whispered, voice atremble. "*You* did. The hauntings. The torment. And you shall suffer every day for it. You deserve your gilded cage, and you will die in it if it's the last thing I do."

The queen rushed forward and snapped the lid shut, nearly catching the girl's finger. A thump sounded against the lid as if the queen had taken a perch atop it. The little girl stifled a cry and nestled down into the stuffy blankets, looking for comfort against the dark.

The queen would leave eventually. Or her mother would come looking. She wouldn't be left inside the trunk. She just had to stay quiet and not let the queen or monsters hear her. Because even after all the things her umi had told her about the monstrous queen, there was one thing the little girl knew for sure.

She did not want to become one of the voices in the dark.

CHAPTER SIXTEEN

Dee

The doors to Dee's bedchambers burst open, and she fell back against Vawk. Bruella stormed in, gold-dipped mace raised high. The same mask of uncertainty flitted across her sister's face, though newfound determination set her lips. Her braids only brushed against the small of her upper back, their tips frayed and choppy as if cut by a blade.

Had she severed her sacred hair to free herself from an attack?

Dee swallowed hard, choking on the pulse ramming against her throat.

"Bruella, I helped you earlier," she sputtered and drew toward the far side of the room, anxiously leading her older sister away from where her younger hid, scared in the dark.

"Why do you think I'm here?" Bruella spat, eyes flashing a rich green. The shade had always been closest to their mother's, the emerald hue unequivocally more beautiful than Qadira's peridot green.

What would their mother think of them now? Though the woman knew what was coming and still chose to birth nine. *To ensure Ahmar's ruler will have strength and fortitude,* she had always said. Dee had drunk up such nonsense as a little child, but now that she was living through what that meant, it seemed absurd and cruel.

"Not a week ago, we sat under the same blankets and read stories to Ma," Dee said, stomach aching.

The memory of laughing and laying on her sister's shoulder felt a million years old, blurry and faint, and nearly unreal. It was a rare occurrence, but their love of stories and their need to pretend they weren't a family slated for death every so often brought the two together.

Dee swallowed and forced herself to keep her sister's gaze. "Does that mean nothing?"

"It has to mean nothing," Bruella snapped, though doubt flickered in pink crystals across her sister's eyes. "I don't want to die."

Dee clenched her jaw and focused on the now. "So you come to kill your savior?"

"Savior?" Bruella laughed, a mad, unhinged trill that set Dee on edge. "You spared me then so you could kill me later. Do you think I don't know that? You saw me as the weaker sibling, the one who could never survive, and set upon the real threats."

"I—" Dee furrowed her brow. "What? You ran. Escaped. I tried to follow, but Icha was trying to throw a knife into my back. I don't want to kill anyone"

"Ha!" Bruella snarked, though pink dappled her eyes with uncertainty. "Ha..." She shook her head, strands of frayed hair slipping free from the severed braid, then she lunged.

Bruella swung her mace hard. Dee ducked, but the metal swiped her left ear. The gold burned furiously against her skin. Dee dodged a second swipe and took a burn on her shoulder. Pain rolled through the wound and down into the muscle. She caught the mace by its handle as it plunged toward her face. The gold pushed closer, and her hands slipped up the wood, burning as they reached the top. Sweat poured into her eyes and down the sides of her nose.

Let me help you and find release, Kakkab hissed, *or you'll get yourself killed and me trapped in this rock's disgusting-smelling dirt for who knows how long.*

"No!" Dee found the strength to shove Bruella back and slip out of the mace's path.

Bruella advanced again, corralling Dee toward the trunk. She shook her head, unwilling to do anything that might release the demon. Sweat dampened her hair, Kakkab's snarling her thoughts. She dipped to the side and around a pillar where the mace clattered, striking sparks.

Bruella flew at her with a shrieking streak of gold and purple and red. The stinging of sweat and tears in Dee's eyes, the metal burning her skin, and Kakkab's blistering condemnations lit the sparks of anger inside her.

"Stop," she growled.

Her silky pants caught the edge of a chair and slowed her down. Dee ripped her leg free with a tear, and Bruella attacked.

Dee balled her fists and threw them up just as Bruella struck. A zulfiqar appeared in her hand, the polearm's split end catching the blow just in time.

Surprise flashed through Bruella's eyes. She yanked her mace back and stared at the weapon that had appeared in Dee's hands. Dee stared, too.

"Witch."

"I'm no witch," Dee snapped, heart racing.

Are you not?

She twitched, wanting to drop the magical weapon, its wooden handle buzzing warm in her palm, but that would leave her open to another attack.

Bahamut's breath, she was tired of her family trying to kill her, but when it was the one older sibling who she had a small relationship with, the betrayal felt worse. So much worse. No wonder Icha and Hulon and Nazdael had always kept their distance.

Dee flashed her eyes up to her sister's. "The demon blade appeared unbidden. I didn't ask for it."

You're rather unappreciative of my gifts.

Dee winced and whispered, "That's because all your gifts bring death."

No, your sister brings death. I bring salvation. All you have to do afterward to thank me is let me go.

"How can I trust anything you say after what you did to Lahm?" Bruella shifted the mace in her hand, knuckles white from their grip. "And why are you acting so strange?"

"Strange?" Dee's brow lifted unbidden. "We're sister princesses who used to fight over hair brushes and now fight to the death with maces to be queen. What is normal? And it's not what you think...the whole thing with Lahm..."

"I don't want to know," Bruella snapped, jabbing the mace at her, not close enough to strike. Fear blackened her beautiful eyes and turned her lips into a trembling snarl. "I don't want to know anything. It just makes it harder."

"To kill?" Dee asked, the words scratching.

Bruella's ugliness dropped into the desperate look of a wounded animal. "I didn't want this. I never wanted this."

"None of us did."

Dee wanted to reach out and stroke her sister's uneven hair, but she kept her fist clenched tight around the ribbon-wrapped handle of the zulfiqar. The weight of it both comforted and disturbed. She didn't want to use it. But she would. She knew this now. Her soul instinctually kept her from killing, and her body instinctually from dying. She was at war with her family. She was at war with herself.

There was no way to win without losing. To lose without winning.

Kakkab chuckled, a deep and menacing mirth that rattled her bones and raised the hairs on her arm and neck. *Delicious.*

Dee shook her head at the voice in her ear. "You are cruel to mock my situation."

"The situation makes a mockery of us all." Bruella tightened her grip on the mace, the wood creaking beneath her fingers. "A forced cage of death that none of us escape."

Dee pursed her lips, sweat soaking into the ribbons of her hooked blade. Moments ticked by. Then degrees.

Finally, Dee whispered, "What if we could?"

"Ha."

"No, really," Dee took a step forward.

Bruella's eyes widened.

Dee retreated, holding the zulfiqar out to the side. "I mean it. What if we could find a way out?"

"You know the rules." Bruella scoffed. "The only way out is death."

Dee scrunched her brows, trying to think like Lahm.

Her voice softened, catching in her throat. "Maybe we don't. Maybe we could rule together, you and I and anyone who survives. Are we not the heirs to the throne? Could we not decide for ourselves how the game is played?"

"I don't want to rule this country. It is cruel." Bruella's face cracked, pink breaking through the black in her eyes. "I don't want to sit on the throne knowing the blood that runs beneath it. I want to be free of this place. But I don't want to die."

She's not wrong, two-footed tantrum. The kind thing to do would be to give her the freedom she seeks with a swift death. The zulfiqar will fly true if you choose to throw it. Or if your stomach is still too weak, call my magic directly. I'll thank you with the swift end of your piteous sister. And you can thank me with my release. Quick, someone must die. You don't have much time.

"Time?" Dee asked, falling for the demon's lure once more.

She clenched her eyes shut and pushed out the lingering sizzle of his words in her mind. She bit her lip, thinking so hard it hurt.

Kakkab couldn't be right, could he? Could Bruella? Was there no way out?

Doubt saturated her heart, soup soaked up in a dry crust of bread. She was not Lahm; she wouldn't win the Allaedam and she couldn't rally a cause. She didn't inspire confidence or walk around the hallways with her head held high. Hulon had been right. She lived in the shadows as a shadow herself. A ghost that lived. She flashed her eyes open and raised them to Bruella's anxious stare. A smile played on the corner of her lips.

"What if everyone thought you were dead?"

Bruella's brow furrowed, but for the first time, the mace in her hand drooped. "What do you mean?"

Dee wasn't quite sure what she meant. The bits and pieces of answers still formed in her mind.

"We stage your death. A fire in your rooms like crazy King Malqum or something. Leave traces of you in your bed so it's believable while you hide in the palace and wait until the Allaedam lifts. Then you can escape through the tunnels underneath. I'll do the same. Stage something crazy and throw my blood about if I have to. Then we can escape together. We two and whoever else wants to be free."

Black cleared from Bruella's eyes, the sweet shimmering blue of hope taking its place. "You'd do that? Help me escape?"

A mistake. Kakkab's warning chilled Dee's lungs and made it hard to breathe. *Someone must die. There is only one target easier than she. What are you afraid of more?*

Dee blanched, knowing she was the easier target the bloodthirsty being spoke of. And while hope had appeared deep in her heart that maybe she, too, could escape, she felt a sense of loss far deeper.

She would not make it through the Allaedam. Whether her death came by Hulon's hands, Nazdael's magic, or the appetite of the wicked essence trapped in her earring, it made no difference.

She locked stares with her sister. "I promise."

As you wish, weak little walker.

Dee bit her cheek and tightened every muscle in her body, waiting for pain or death or whatever the creature had in mind. She only hoped to survive Kakkab's wrath long enough to fulfill her promise.

A clatter sounded behind her.

She startled and spun around. Sadie had tumbled from the curtain and lay strewn on the bed, purple face tinted a deep bluish plum.

Bruella gasped. "Is that—"

Dee's eyes widened, and she dashed toward the trunk. "Chiba!"

CHAPTER SEVENTEEN

The Khadim

The khadim scuttled into Qadira's bedchamber, eyes glued to the floor and heart pounding in his brain. Why today of all days? If he hadn't been late... If he hadn't stopped by to flirt with that brown-eyed maid with dimpled cheeks on the floor below before making it to his station....

His job was to light the sconces in the hallway with his pure-white fire. To roll up the rugs, beat them, and return them to their hallways. To occasionally help a maid or older manservant carry filth out of the palace. But this? He'd never set a step in Qadira's bedchambers a day in his life. He wasn't usually allowed to even breathe in the same hallway. And it was a long hallway to hold his breath down.

But today, that didn't seem to matter. He had heard the royal screeches bounding off the marble three galleries over, but it had been the first time he had heard such ungodly sounds. Not the case for all the other servants. The moment her shrill screams had permeated the peace of the City of Pearls, every breathing soul had vanished. Inside brocade curtains. Behind vases and urns. He even watched a maid scurry underneath a bed. But not him. He still had dimples and sparkling eyes on his mind, and as he stared agape at the instant vanishing of a hundred manservants as if into thin air, he had been spotted by the queen.

She hadn't said a word, eyes blazing brighter than Ursa Major on a clear night. She just clacked over in her sharp heels, grabbed his arm in a grip akin to the hold of death, and dragged him into her chamber.

He squirmed the instant his feet sank into the plush carpet. He had heard from golden-haired Johann, the queen's usual carnal flavor of choice, about the whims of the queen, especially since she had started trying to get pregnant. Her needs were frequent... and anything but gentle. Deep scratches frequented Johann's back, and his lip was always bleeding. But if she had Johann, what did the purportedly cruel queen want from a mere khadim? He was an average *whakim*. Nothing to look at, but nothing to sneeze at either. And he had only been working at the palace for two weeks. Johann was the purple version of the Ardish Adonis.

"Boy," Queen Qadira snapped, her bright red nails catching the light. "If I have to catch your attention one more time, it will be with hot irons in your retinas."

He nodded vigorously. Then changed to a shake, stuttering something he hoped was right. He may be new, but Qadira's consistency in following through on her threats was well-established: one hundred percent. And her threats were always whatever whimsical torture crawled its way into her mind that day. Rarely orthodox, her victims—transgressors—could only pray that her tongue was tired the day she lashed out at them so her threats would be vague and brief.

That rarely happened.

Queen Qadira sneered down her nose at him. "Stop trembling you pathetic pour of pegasus piss."

The Khadim winced. "Sorry, Your Royal...ness."

"Ew." She grimaced, her bony frame curling in. "I did not call you into my sacred chambers to speak. You will remove the trunk in the corner and burn it on the top parapet of the palace."

"On the royal funeral pyre?" The Khadim asked, his fat tongue not listening.

Her eyes flashed green, illuminating the room in an eerie light and sending shivers down his spine. "What did I say about speaking? You're lucky Vawk isn't present to hear my decree you be torn apart by *marleki* in a storm of swarming Ardish bees.

Your face is grotesque enough as it is, the puss-filled welts of venom would leave your corpse utterly unrecognizable."

The khadim winced.

Qadira's sharp eyes slowly swept his face.

"On the other hand, that may be a blessing. Keep your mouth shut and remove the trunk, and I shall let you choose if you'd prefer to escape your ugly face or continue living with it."

The khadim nodded, his heart thudding in his trembling hands as he slapped them together and bowed. He rushed over to the trunk and grabbed the smooth handle on the side. He braced his back and knees, preparing for an enormous amount of weight. He garnered his strength and heaved. The trunk lifted easily, and he stumbled backward, dragging it with him. The polished wood caught its corner and tilted. His eyes widened, flashing between the tipping trunk and the queen's horrified face.

The trunk crashed on its side, the lid cracking open. He jumped up and rushed forward. She grabbed the collar of his kurta and yanked back so hard, the force bruised his trachea. He fell to the ground sputtering. The queen fell upon the trunk, screaming. She scrambled to drape her robes over the side, then shoved the trunk right-side-up. With trembling hands, she clamped the lid shut, fell upon it, and sobbed.

But not before the khadim saw.

He pressed a hand to his mouth, tears in his eyes as he cried for his life and, strangely, for hers.

"*'ana asf!* I'm sorry, I'm so sorry!"

Her head snapped toward him, eyes the deep black of the sky without stars, of utter and abject terror.

"Get out," she hissed. "Get out!"

He jumped to his feet and stumbled toward the door. He yanked it open and fell out, barely keeping his feet as he pelted away from the crazy queen. He'd have to leave the palace now. There was no way he would wait for the queen to find her tongue and put a bounty on his ugly face. Not after she had stared at it so. Not after what he had seen in her eyes and inside the peeking dark of the trunk.

Not when he wanted to live.

All that lived in that room was the black of death.

THIRD & FOURTH CULLING

A Formal Allaedam Declaration

Formal Declaration of Third and Fourth Allaedam Culling

By the grace and providence of the Celestial Bahamut on the thirty-fifth day of the Seventh Moon's One-Thousandth Shadow Pass, in the time of the Fifteenth Allaedam to secure the throne of Ahmar, two cullings eliminated the weak and chaotic. During the Allaedam, the Eighth Heir of the True Nine who have claim to the throne of Ahmar killed the Fifth and Ninth True Heirs beyond recognition by fire in her bedchambers of the Crystal Palace. Blood Magic confirmed the deaths through a femur found inside a trunk and three fingers found upon the cinders of a rug.

The official record of True Heirs to the Ahmaran throne reads as:

First True Heir, Shutor - Honorably killed by the Third Heir for his country

Second True Heir, Talcum - Honorably killed by the Third Heir for his country

Third True Heir, Hulon - Living at 25 years old

Fourth True Heir, Nazdael - Living at 21 years old

Fifth True Heir, Bruella - Honorably killed by the Eighth Heir for her country

Sixth True Heir, Icha - Honorably killed by the Eighth Heir for her country

Seventh True Heir, Lahmdan - Honorably killed by the Eighth Heir for her country

Eighth True Heir, Qadira - Living at 13 years old

Ninth and final True Heir, Chiba - Honorably killed by the Eighth Heir for her country

No other deaths are yet recorded as the country awaits the victor of the Allaedam, but with the Bahamut as Ahmar's witness, only one heir can rule.

CHAPTER EIGHTEEN

Dee

Dee stared at the flames licking the sky, green against purple, light against light. The contract in her hand felt heavy, somehow, though it was simple parchment and ink.

After Chiba, Bruella had fallen into hysterics, convinced Qadira was luring her into a trap to kill her off, too. And why wouldn't she? Chiba's tiny body, suffocated by blankets and a promise that everything would be okay, was more than Dee could bear. Though she had borne it, the scattered, sharded pieces of herself in a shattered, broken way.

It had taken swearing an oath with a bouquet of taluli in her hands to convince Bruella to trust her long enough to sign the contract—a promise that Qadira would let Bruella hide until the Allaedam was called and then go free. In return, Bruella promised to never vie for the throne or reveal herself as a True Heir after her escape. She disappeared with her bloodservant then, never to be seen again—or so Dee hoped.

Through the negotiations, Dee had remained calm. No... not calm. Hollow. An empty shell as she prepared the fire to hide Bruella's disappearance and destroy the trunk Dee couldn't bare to look at. Her face had moved nary a twitch as she draped the flammable taluli around her bed. As she strewed it across the floor in lazy patterns. As she heaped vines upon Sadie's lifeless body. It wasn't until she had reached the polished wood trunk that was supposed to be Chiba's salvation that Dee's bottom lip had trembled. She laid the end of each twist of taluli blossoms so they started from Chiba and spread outward, innocence, the root of death.

Weakness, the source of demise.

She was tempted to burn herself with the bed, Sadie, Chiba, and Bruella's clothes and weapons, a few chopped-off fingers and blood, but then who would there be to blame? To reward? When the room caught alight and their dust turned to ashes, the nation would need a killer. They required one. And who better than the Eighth True Heir?

So she had lit a single blossom with her lime-green fire and dropped it on the knot on Chiba's chest. Then walked out into the courtyard where Lahm's blood still stained the cobblestone and watched the corner of the palace burn.

A tragedy. Kakkab sounded bored.

Heat from the flames toasted her skin, itchy and hot, but the monster froze her core.

"It didn't have to be," Dee whispered.

The courtyard buzzed with a chaotic mess of guards and servants working to put out the remainder of the fire. They had been at it for at least thirty degrees, trying to stop the spread of destruction as the flames ate up all the taluli in the bedchambers and the vines that clung to the walls, looking for more entry points into the palace.

Kakkab's voice grew indignant. *I certainly agree. If you would just let me help you, we could move on to you being queen and letting me go.*

"Let you go?" She scoffed, cold and hurting. "After what you did to Chiba?"

What I *did?*

"You murdered an innocent child!"

Why is innocence a qualifier for life with you djinn? Five different intentions can all lead to the same end. Making decisions based on feelings and uninformed judgments results in a substantial amount of tedium and poor outcomes.

"Because—" Dee clenched her fists, searching for the right words, the right thoughts. "Because some djinn deserve life more than others."

I daresay djinn are the most inefficient creatures in all of the billions of worlds that contain life. What sliding scale are we using today? Good versus evil? Competent versus idiotic? Strong versus weak? The laws of nature or the laws of djinn?

"All of them," she snapped, limbs shaking. "None of them. I don't know. But Chiba didn't deserve this."

What's done is done, you sublunary sob story. The better question is, what do you deserve?

Dee gritted her teeth. "Vengeance. Vindication."

Victory?

Dee thought about that for a moment. "Yes," she finally replied, a new hunger awakening in the emptiness inside her. "Over you."

Kakkab's laughter stirred, coals of fire in her brain. *You grow inspired, do you? I find that delicious.*

"You must be stopped." She clenched her fist and squeezed her stinging eyes shut. "I don't know how, yet, but when I do, I will end you for what you've done."

What is it you think I've done, dramatic djinn?

"Called weapons into my hands. Encouraged mayhem. Killed my siblings."

As I recall, you pushed your brother out the window. You held the mysterious blade your Icha died on. And it was you, not I, who chose to shove the poor creature into a trunk with no air. Why did you think that was a good idea?

Dee flashed her eyes open, green light spilling into the space around them as horrific images of blue lips and clenched fists infiltrated her mind. "Why did *I*?"

Unless your true intention was to kill your frail little blood relation.

"You're the one I intend to kill!"

"I didn't think you heard me approach," a tenor cut in behind her.

Dee whipped around, heart in her throat. Hulon hovered over her, twice her age and more than that in size. The fire behind her flickered in his bright green eyes and set an orange glow to his cream and purple Ahmaran uniform. Not a trace of blood coated his kaftan. Not a drop dotted his boots. He looked like he just left the *hamam* and was out for a stroll in the courtyard while she looked like a bog beast from a horror story. The contrast sent ice through her veins.

Dee's mind raced, not sure what to say, but the Lahm inside her whispered to keep the advantage.

She swallowed. "You are not so cunning as you think, big brother."

"Brother?" Hulon smirked. "Feeling more familial towards me now that you're out for my blood? Poor Nazdael, she'll be so hurt coming in last."

"She'll live." Dee bristled. "For now."

Hulon chuckled. "I thought the fire that killed Chiba and Bruella was burned solely in your bedchambers. Apparently, I was wrong." He took a step toward her, and she flinched despite herself. His grin widened. "Where's your hairless bloodservant? I enjoy the way he sputters whenever I walk by."

Dee grimaced. Vawk was taking Bruella to the hidden tunnels beneath the palace to hide since she did not have her own bloodservant to lead the way. He also insisted, not convinced Bruella wouldn't change her mind and betray them all.

"If you're intent is to rule, why are you using your words now instead of a knife?" Though her legs felt like jelly, she forced her shoulders straight and met his eyes. "Or are you the real shadow, forcing me to bloody my hands as you wait until the end to slit my throat? Would there be a knife in my back if I hadn't noticed you there?"

"Look at little Dee Dee Ra finding her voice." He scoffed. "Sometimes words are more powerful than knives, sister, when aiming to destroy."

Her gaze wavered, knowing that had to be true. The demon in her ear, now conspicuously silent, was a testament to that.

"And gaining the kingship is just part of the goal." He stepped up beside her, each facing a different way, so he could whisper in her ear. "What ruler would our people prefer? The killer of a child, or the man who killed the killer?"

She blanched, the heat of the fire against her back. "So you are playing shadow, making me look like a villain so you can ascend as a hero?" The words caught in her throat.

"Precisely."

Kakkab cackled, though it was muted and quiet like he was afraid Hulon could hear him.

"Then the work is done," she choked. "Only Nazdael remains, and she's older and fiercer than I. Just stab me now and stop pretending." Dee turned and faced Hulon, her neck craning to match his gaze in such close quarters. She could smell taluli and spice on his shirt.

Hulon bent closer, his nose touching the side of hers. "No."

Dee balled her fists. "Why not?"

You're upset he won't kill you?

"Because you want me to."

"I—You—" Heat filled her face. "This isn't a game, Hulon."

He stood and tilted his head, eyes fiery and keen. "That's exactly what it is."

"Says you. You and all the stupid guards making bets and the peasants in the kingdom and—" She bit off Kakkab's name. "To me, it's lives. It's family. It's... our souls."

"Hmm." Hulon touched a hand to his chin. "And what if someone else agreed with me? What if someone else was hiding in the shadows, waiting for you to finish so they could take the throne?"

"Nazdael?" She scrunched her nose and shook her head. "She's always been reclusive, hiding away with her magic powders and books. I haven't even seen her in a year. For all anyone knows, she died in her bookshelves months ago before all this started."

He chuckled, and that made her feel worse than anything. "You're not wrong. She's been difficult to locate. But I wasn't talking about her."

"Then who?"

"Your other half."

Her eyes snapped to his, hope and desperation and yearning and anger all boiling up inside her.

Recognition passed through his glittering gaze. "I've piqued your interest."

"He can't be alive. I'd know if he were. I'd know."

"Like you knew about the fire below Ma's window?"

"Of course, I knew about it. I started it to distract the guards so we could climb the wall."

Hulon's smile reflected the fire. "He had you do that, too, huh? He's more clever than I thought, keeping his hands clean while his shadow did his work."

"What are you talking about?" Dee snapped, patience wearing thin.

"Taluli smoke attaches to the lungs and feeds. Ma was already sick and weakened with the *famels*. Even a pipeful of taluli smoke would have killed her. And you two lit a fire full of them directly below her window, then blew it high with Quwian seeds. Lahmdan is cunning. He knew what it would do. He knew it would kill Ma and start the Allaedam."

Qadira shook her head, blinking her eyes against the heat and Hulon's accusation.

"He didn't know. He would have told me. He would have warned me."

"Would he?" Hulon faked a pitiful face.

Dee's heart raced. Lahmdan wouldn't have led her into the Allaedam unprepared. They were looking for solutions. For ways to keep safe. He wanted to rule with her, to keep her safe. The taluli blossom told her so.

The same blossoms that killed Ma.

"You jest." She snapped her eyes to his, doubt in the only person she ever trusted curdling her blood. "You're just trying to break me so you can have your heroic takeover. Lahmdan didn't kill Ma on purpose. And he can't— He can't be—" Her head swam, recalling events through the smokey veil of sorrow. "I saw him fall. I saw him bleed."

"And then you disappeared, little coward, unable to take the horrified adulation that turned your way for even a moment. Not even when you served your nation so nobly."

"Nobly?"

Dee clenched her fists harder, and a cold handle appeared in her hand. She whipped the new blade around and pressed it against Hulon's stomach, fury raging through her.

He leaned in, so the sparkling dagger pierced through his shirt and dimpled his skin.

"Your turn, *sister*."

Sweat broke out across her forehead.

Kakkab remained silent.

Her hand twitched on the black onyx, the firelight turning the blade a ghastly green.

She readjusted her grip. Glanced between the challenge in Hulon's eyes and the weapon pressing into his flesh. Then yanked it away.

I starve, and you remain weak.

She dropped the blade with a clatter.

"I'm not a murderer. I'm not." Not the way everyone thought she was, despite Chiba's lifeless body hovering hauntingly in her mind. And she wasn't Lahm, either. Because he would have sunk the blade deep in Hulon's stomach and thought it noble, too.

Wouldn't he?

And what did that mean about Ma's death?

She buried her face in her hands and squeaked out the question burning on her tongue. "Lahm isn't still alive... is he?"

CHAPTER NINETEEN
The Mafya

THE MAFYA CONSIGLIERE WALKED into the throne room, noting the changes. It had been nearly forty-four years since she last walked under the crystal dome, and in that time red-veined marble had replaced the blue, all the curtains had been torn down, and a coating of noxious glitter dusted the columns, concealing any battle wounds in the centuries-old marble. Not a servant or guard lined the room, and an unsettling chill filled the air.

She nearly laughed. Now that she thought about it, it wasn't that much different than the last time she had been in there at all.

What had changed the most was how much the little queen had grown.

Qadira was taller now, though no fuller. She wore bright red lipstick where once her natural pink had shown through. And her gaze held something distant and cold that had not been a part of her before. The cost of surviving a massacre. The consigliere knew that look well.

The consigliere adjusted the leather strap that crisscrossed over her shoulders and tugged at the folds of her cerulean scarf. It smelled strangely familiar in the airy palace, though she couldn't place the scent at first. It wasn't roses or lilies, though the perfume had hints of both. Not lilacs or lavender, either. She scrunched her nose and pushed forward, the gentle swish of her silk pants the only sound in the open room. Then it hit her. The scent was taluli, the blossom that used to run rampant across the palace before Qadira burned them all down.

Normally, audiences with rulers didn't bother her. Why would they? She ruled the underworld of the most powerful city this side of the Seventh Moon's arc, and all without having to get her hands dirty. The perks of being the whisper in the boss's ear instead of owning it. Ears could be cut off. So could fingers, for that matter. That's why she always kept her remaining fingers wrapped in soft lambskin with djinn-burning brass knuckles studded in the top.

Qadira was different from other rulers. Their relationship was. Her roots started in Qadira. Corruption from deception. Success from compromise. Qadira made her. She saved her. And now, after all these years, she had called her to the throne.

Which was exactly where the glittering queen sat, a glass bead choker propping her head up because that's the only way the enormous crystal crown didn't snap her thin, little neck. The six diamonds on top flashed at the consigliere with each step. She looked away and sniffed, rubbing her nose across the back of her sleeve.

When she arrived in front of her majesty, she swept her kurta back into a bow and knelt. "Your Triumph."

"El Alnaaji," Qadira replied. "It has been a long time."

"I did not think I'd be welcome back."

A tiny smile brushed Qadira's lips. "Neither did I."

"You've redecorated the place," El Anaaji said, taking in the painful glamour. "Covered everything up."

"Would you prefer I lay everything bare?

El Anaaji clenched her jaw, the threat clear.

She stood. "May I ask what calls me to your feet? I've stayed out of your way as requested. Benefited the crown with mutually profitable exploits. Kept crime down and away from the gates of the palace. Have I not served you honorably?"

"You have." Qadira titled her head to the right almost imperceptibly, though the movement was enough to shoot shimmers of reflected light across the room. "It is your loyalty that has caught my attention. You see, I require something that is not easily attainable."

El Enaaji stroked a finger along her jaw. "It's not another Ghaluman warlord, is it? I hear you already have your hooks in one of those."

"It didn't work out." Qadira's lip curled.

"Didn't put up with your short-tempered grandstanding?"

Qadira smirked. "Not even a little."

"Good for him." El Enaaji flashed a grin. "And good for you."

"What do you mean?"

"I know the look in those green eyes. I think you like him."

Qadira narrowed her gaze. "Not a chance."

"Or the perfect chance." El Anaaji risked a step closer. "Why not give the warlord a chance?"

"Because he's an insufferable know-it-all who was born in the sand and wants everything his way."

El Anaaji laughed. "There are worse things than an entitled ruler who wants their way all the time, don't you think? Those are a dinar a dozen."

"Too true." Qadira sighed and lifted the crown from her head, placing it on the arm of the glittering throne.

She slid her hand beneath her long black braid and rubbed her neck, tilting her head from side to side. The action pushed El Anaaji a step back. Qadira looked tired then. Weary and wary and a little bit beat, like any other djinn who couldn't find a way out of the pit they found themselves in. More like a sister and less like a queen.

El Anaaji swallowed and took a risk. "What's the real problem? You don't let anyone bring you down, and you appreciate strength."

Her lime-green eyes raised to El Anaaji's, so similar to her own. "I need a baby and he refuses to grant me one."

El Anaaji barked out a laugh, then slapped a hand over her mouth.

Qadira stared yellow-rimmed daggers at her. "Something funny?"

"My apologies," El Anaaji dipped down low, cursing herself for acting familiar. For remembering more than forgetting. "I just—You're Queen Qadira, the Glamour of Ahmar. You're smart, and cunning, and gorgeous. Find another man. One far less moon-burnt than a Ghaluman chieftain with his bare chest and desire for war."

"You don't understand." Qadira's bright lips slipped into an uncharacteristic pout. "I have to have him."

"Why?"

"Because!" Qadira slapped her hand on the throne, then curled her fingers in tight. She cleared her throat. "Because I do. I'm on a deadline, and I need him to marry me by the end of the month."

"That's days away," El Anaaji nearly spit. "A Ghaluman's more likely to wade through a Zabriyan snowstorm than they are to be bullied into something."

"I'm well aware," Qadira looked up, eyes cold and lips in a smirk. "Why do you think I called you, little diplomat?"

El Anaaji balked. "Diplomat? I coax criminals into staying out of trouble and giving me what I want. I'd hardly say—"

"I was referring to your younger days when your tongue was silkier than my sheets."

El Anaaji swallowed, her throat suddenly parched. "Qadira—"

"Get it done or we'll both be in trouble."

"But why me?" El Anaaji tempted the queen's wrath. She had to. Such a high-profile job led to the risk of exposure, and that was the last thing she wanted. "You have so many other more qualified people to do this, even with my past. Because of my past."

"I know the risk," Qadira quipped. "But you look like me, minus your full chest and wide hips."

"What?"

"Just do as you're told, like everyone else."

Her words stung, and El Anaaji scowled. "Sis—"

"Enough!" Qadira stood, her frame trembling under the heavens. A crystal dagger glowed in her hand, appearing as if out of the air, a light green aura about it that sent chills down El Anaaji's spine. "Don't push me. You don't know what I've been through. What I can do."

"As you wish," El Anaaji bowed and backed away, rubbing her thumb over her missing fingers, reminding her why she obeyed.

The task would be impossible, but what else could she say? She only lived because Qadira let her, and that could change at any moment. Anyway, she'd rather rule the underworld than the throne of Ahmar. There were far fewer people who wanted to slit her throat.

She pressed her palms together and bowed. "Anything else, my Queen?"

"There is." Qadira took her crown and placed it back on her head, lifting her chin to reveal her slender neck. She smiled, and the gems shone brightly under the crystal dome overhead. "I need a meeting with a star."

CHAPTER TWENTY

Dee

In answer to Dee's question, Hulon shrugged with a smirk and left her to watch the destruction her hands had created. For the second time.

Had she really killed Ma by executing Lahm's plan? Had he known what would happen the whole time?

Then again, that was Lahm's plan for her, wasn't it? To look weak and incompetent so no one saw her as a threat.

She pinched the bridge of her nose, hands shaking.

We don't want you to look competent. We want you to look weak so everyone's guard will be down when they approach.

Dee slid her way to the edge of the courtyard behind the *yetollamae* bushes and pressed her back against the cold stone.

But if Lahm had used her as his shadow as Hulon said, then she wasn't *appearing* incompetent and weak. She *was* those things.

Dee shook her head hard and looked up at the window where she and Lahm had climbed. He wouldn't do that to her. He wouldn't use her. He wanted to rule with her. The taluli blossoms said so.

She closed her eyes, took a deep breath, and thought of Lahm. Of his tender smile and kind eyes. Of his words of wisdom and lies about the taluli fire. Love and frustration mingled with his image. Fire ignited in her blood and tugged at the space between both worlds. She tried to apparate to him but nothing happened. Hot tears moistened her eyelids as she tried again. And again. And again. And again.

Angry and shaking, she slumped against the wall.

"Hulon, you liar," she growled through clenched teeth.

Problem, bipedal?

"Not for you to weigh in on."

Are your little royal djinn powers not working? Remind me what that means again.

She snarled and punched her fist back against the stone wall. Then glanced up at the window high above. The room of a crazed king that had started this all. The room protected by charms so a djinn could easily escape but not easily enter.

Dee narrowed her eyes, pulse picking up. What if Hulon wasn't lying? What if Lahm lived, hiding in the place he wanted to be their home base? What he rested above her now, waiting for her to return?

Dee wiped her nose on her sleeve. With nothing to lose and the knowledge of how to use her legs and stay close to the stone, she made quick work up the side. When she reached the top, she slid inside, stepping where scattered footprints already marked the dust.

Not the venue I was hoping for.

"I thought you might be missing home."

This is not my home, you masochistic mortal.

Dee breathed in the stale air, the dusty particles catching the firelight outside so they flickered in shades of orange and red.

"And how would I know that, being? You tell me nothing."

Nothing is free.

"Including your freedom."

I offer you help in exchange for releasing what was not yours, to begin with.

She shot a glare at her earring. "You offer death."

To kill as you direct. To make you queen. To keep order in your kingdom.

"To steal my soul. But I don't need your help with that. I've caused death with your aid."

Have you, witch? Are you ready to recognize your role as my devout?

Dee traced Lahm's name carefully in the soot, thinking over all that happened since she had stared up at the First Moon that morning.

"You gave me that knife to kill Icha."

A cursed piece from a small tribe in the Tibetan mountains on Ard that always finds its mark. The perfect tool to fight a knife-thrower. It's a shame you dropped that one.

She winced. "And Chiba..." Dee bit her lip. "You told me to put her in that trunk."

I did nothing of the sort. I simply said I'd have great use for it after you asked. And I did.

The pit in her stomach opened wide, leaving her sick. "You knew she'd die in there."

I certainly hoped, but it was your choice.

Any remaining rage disappeared into the black hole inside her. "And Lahm. You said I'd regret not letting you out... And then Lahm fell out the window. Did you do that? Make me trip and fall into him so he died, too?"

I—

A popping sounded from the empty room to Dee's left. She jumped to her feet, the cavern in her chest pounding, drowning out what Kakkab whispered. Purple smoke curled around the corner, filling up the bechambers. Coughing, Dee pressed a hand to her mouth and stumbled onto her knees.

The air's clearer down here. Stay low, Kakkab hissed, *and apparate.*

Dee nodded, knowing she'd end up back in the blue-veined marble hallway by the throne room. She closed her eyes and tried to pinch her fire between worlds toward Vawk but was met with a solid wall.

She screeched in frustration and dug her nails into the black floor. Her mind raced over what could be happening, but it wasn't until a bell-adorned slipper stepped out into the smoke that Dee realized.

Nazdael.

What better place for her to hide than the abandoned room that already resulted in the death of one heir? Dee had climbed right into the spider's nest. She was under attack once again, and from the very vantage point that Lahm had wanted for their own. Her frayed nerves unraveled more, slipping into panic.

"Qadira?" Nazdael's alto called through the peach-smelling smoke. "Reveal yourself. I know you're there."

Dee clenched her fist, trying again and again to conjure a blade.

"Kakkab!" she gasped.

Hm?

"I'm going to die."

You might.

"So, do the thing!"

Thing?

She growled and scurried on her hands and knees away from the tinkling slippers that moved gracefully through the purple cloud. "I need a weapon."

You're the witch.

"Qadira!" Nazdael snapped again. The bells on her feet paused their wandering. "Stop this cowardice and face me."

Dee backed up, looking for the window in anxious glances over her shoulder. Nazdael was close enough now, the glint of a silver blade with a hilt wrapped in blue leather winked at her next to her sister's silk dress. Her bell slippers moved slowly, deliberately—Nazdael searching for the sounds she heard in the room.

"Give me a weapon," Dee whispered, a mix between a snap and a plead.

I refuse to do all the work. You can call on my magic and produce one yourself. You have before.

She tightened her jaw. "How?"

Simple. You just need murder in your heart.

"I don't—"

Nazdael's sharp voice cut her off. "Stand, Qadira! I know it is you who has come for my life."

Dee stayed crouched, tucking her knees closer to her body and wrapping her arms around them. She held her breath and eyed the approaching bells. Their soft *tinkling* carried through the glittering smoke, setting her nerves on edge.

"I said stand!" Nazdael screeched.

Dee shot up, pressing her back against the wall. Her pulse pounded in her neck, and her breaths came in short, painful bursts. She stared wide-eyed at Nazdael. Her older sister's long hair brushed her calves, braided in thick leather straps of a sparkling blue that shimmered like the night sky. Her dress matched, a dark kiss on her light-purple skin. Dark red stained her frowning lips.

"There you are." Nazdael tilted her head, little bells in her ears jingling to match her feet. "Congratulations."

"For what?"

Dee clenched her fist, wishing for a weapon, but she had to want to kill to get help from the being, or so he said. Could that be true? She hadn't wanted to kill Icha or Bruella, had she? What about Hulon in the courtyard? She had conjured the weapon then, too, but had let him live.

"For finding me before Hulon," Nazdael quipped. "He's been trying ever so desperately."

Dee nodded slowly. "He's hoping I'll kill you for him."

Nazdael's bright red lips twitched. "And is that your plan?"

"That depends on you." Dee bit her bottom lip, still clenching and unclenching her fists behind her back. "Do you want to kill me?"

Her sister narrowed her bright eyes and tapped her chin with a slender finger. "Want has anything to do with it. Unless you're Hulon, perhaps. I simply need you to die so that I may live."

The thundering in Dee's ears lessened. Perhaps Nazdael could be reasoned with like Bruella. Perhaps this could be her own out. A way to disappear and give the victory to Nazdael. A way to make up for her accident with Lahm. She didn't want to rule without him either. Which meant she never could.

Not this again, Kakkab groaned.

She swallowed and outstretched a hand. "If you don't want to, you don't have to."

I refuse to take part in these ridiculous parlays.

"I'm listening." Nazdael raised her leather-bound dagger and pressed the broad side of the blade against her lip.

Smoke and stars reflected in the silver, but not Qadira. Not the room or the glimmer of the sky outside. Just green and dark and the cosmos, and a winking shimmer right where her ear would be.

Kakkab gasped, a sharp inhale that sent chills down Dee's spine. *Someone will die now, underwhelming urchin. You decide who. But you will not survive this match without me.*

"I shan't have a match at all," Dee muttered, straightening her shoulders with newfound confidence. Kakkab was scared she'd find a way to survive the Allaedam without him and never give him release. "I'm winning, and I don't need your help."

You can't do anything without someone dying. Not when that witch wields more power than you. Would you rather use my power and choose who dies or leave it to chance like with little Chiba... or worse?

Before Dee could summon an answer, Nazdael's eyes widened. "You little witch." Her lips fell into a sneer.

"I—" Qadira threw herself to the side as the cosmic dagger flew at her.

The shining metal sunk easily into the grooves of the stone wall behind her, its handle reverberating from the force. Dee shot wide eyes at her sister. "Why did you do that?"

"To kill you," Nazdael said, voice tight and resigned.

Dee sputtered. "What about our deal?"

"It seems you've already made one."

Dee shook her head. "I don't understand."

She means with me, you querulous queen.

Her hand darted up to the earring, glowing warmer now. "I didn't do anything."

Nazdael dipped her head to one side, almost birdlike. Her long hair swept the floor, earrings ringing. "It all makes sense, cold-blooded murder coming from meek little Qadira. Ba. Lahmdan. Icha and Bruella. Even sweet Chiba." Her forehead creased. "You cheated."

Indignation bloomed in Dee's chest, hot and sticky. "I didn't kill anyone in cold blood. They were accidents. I didn't cheat. Or, I did with Bruella, but not in the way you think."

Nazdael rushed forward in a wisp of smoke, smashing her hand into the wall next to Qadira's face. The glitter swam about them, stinging her eyes.

Nazdael's shining eyes bore into Qadira's, her breathing heavy and fast. "Accidents don't happen when you sell your soul to a star."

She ripped the dagger from the wall and sliced down.

Pain tore into Qadira's clavicle and down under her right arm, snapping the thin bone as it went. Dee screamed and pushed her way past, stumbling into the purple smoke. Stabbing agony clouded her mind and set her bones shaking. Her arm no longer responded, and all the heat in the room had drained to a freezing cold, made worse by the sweat dripping from her skin.

Let me protect you, Kakkab screeched, tearing at her mind. *Let me make you queen and be free.*

"No," Qadira gasped. "I can't trust you or anyone."

Another swipe slashed into her back, Nazdael's silver burning her flesh with a noxious smell. Stumble. Cut. Scream. And Kakkab's angry snarls.

It didn't matter. Nothing she did could make the blade appear in her hand. Nazdael moved as if a ghost, her advances faster than light, her swipes invisible aside from the swirl of peach-smelling smoke that billowed out of each arc's path.

"How is she so fast?" Qadira spat blood and raced through the fog.

Her hands hit a wall, and she followed it down, unable to see where she was going. When she felt like she was out of the reach of Nazdael long enough to stand still, she stopped and tried to apparate. Her fire refused to ignite, to even throw her through the scrape of magical corridors and dump her near the throne room.

The witch blocks your fire, keeping you contained. It does not feel so good to be trapped, does it, haughty hominid.

Qadira sank against the wall. "Why? How? How is she so fast? How does she block my powers so easily?"

She's a witch. She's made a deal with a Celestial, just like you.

Dee wiped feverishly at the sweat burning her eyes. Did strange voices push Nazdael to do terrible things as well? Was she tormented by a voice that betrayed her goodness and pushed her toward evil? For Kakkab had so far brought her torment.

He had also helped keep her alive on more than one occasion. But that was the crux of the matter. She wasn't sure she did want to live. Not past the instincts that coursed through her veins and compelled her muscles to move. To dodge and swipe and run, so she could remain breathing.

She knew, if nothing else, she didn't want to live in Ahmar. Not like this. Not as queen.

And if that was the case, and Nazdael refused to negotiate, why *did* she keep running? If she faced her sister's blade, either she would die, or Nazdael would. That's what Kakkab said, right? That one of them must die. Either way, the problem would solve itself.

Dee stopped in her tracks, nearly toppling over, and turned, arms stretched out once more.

What are you doing?

"Ending this."

By dying? Kakkab roared.

"By forcing a fate, one way or another."

You little—

Nazdael smashed through the smoke like a hammer, eyes glowing green and red lips undeniably sad. Her silver blade whipped through the purple haze, glowing with starlight. It struck, hot and bright.

But not in Qadira's flesh. Not in her muscle or her bones. Not even through the sacred ties of her hair.

Dee fell back, arms crisscrossing her body, and hit the floor. Why no pain? No tearing and burning and aching in her nerves?

A ripple shivered through her body, and she looked up at Lahm.

CHAPTER TWENTY-ONE

The Eternal Witch of Finding

PASHA WAS SEVEN YEARS into her ten-year sentence—punishment for failing to fulfill a contract she had made with her patron Celestial to enslave a pesky prince. She had asked for leniency from Ursa major, having served the great star as the devout Eternal Witch of Finding for nearly seven decades, but it mattered little. Stars were fickle beings, as easily entertained as they were enraged, as enraptured as they were bored. Such is the way of immortals.

The stars demanded a cost for their more powerful magic, and Pasha wanted to be powerful. Sometimes, that meant being at the beck-and-call of a haughty star for a decade.

But breaking free from such powerful prison sentences required cunning and patience and a bit of will and whim. So it was that Pasha rolled out of bed when a strange woman with lime green eyes and missing fingers knocked on her door. She had stretched and yawned, ready to fry whoever thought it decent to make house calls when the Fourth Moon was at its highest point in the sky, blessing both ne'er-do-wells and lovers alike. But the paths one least expects are often the ones that pay out the most. And the strange visit from a high-ranking member of the mafya promised to prove her theory right.

The woman turned out to be a messenger from the queen herself—or so she claimed—seeking something even harder to believe. A meeting with Pisces—the grumpy Celestial of Life who had little patience for the very mortals his powers helped create. Pasha had only dealt with him a few times, and every time, he proved himself to be exactly as difficult as the rumors said him to be.

Pasha laughed El Anaaji off at first, but something in the request intrigued her, whispering that this may be her chance to gain freedom. Why would the Queen of Ahmar, who was well-known for her bloodied hands, be seeking life at all?

She summoned her Finding Fire the moment the woman left, gathering heather and jade, lavender and *hitchwitch* and lighting them all with a gentle push of heat. The fragrant smoke drew her mind to the stars, and she cast a magic line. With held breath, she waited for it to catch.

The fire hook sunk into Ursa's lustrous magic, and, with a quick tug, Pasha flung her minds-eye toward it. Her magic swished past galaxies she knew well and a few she did not until her mind existed within the aura of Ursa Major. The space her being occupied felt like the bottom of a volcano, an intense heat that tasted like metallic cotton. She laid any useless thoughts to the side and allowed the star's power to fill her up. Technically, she wasn't supposed to be using Ursa's stronger magic when not on a job, but the Celestial had been rather demanding lately and wouldn't find out if Pasha slipped a few searches into the fray. Probably.

It was worth the risk.

Pasha started with questions about the stranger at her door and why the woman—who lacked the fear of death in her eyes that so often accompanied Qadira's servants—was working on her Royal Temper Tantrum's behalf. Answer: El Anaaji, or "The Survivor" to native tongues, was far more than a high-ranking mafya thug. The little royal imposter was owed something akin to a debt of life.

Next, Pasha dove into why the Queen of Ahmar, known for killing life, not curating it, was seeking a favor from the very Celestial who created it. It's not like Pisces owed the queen money.

Pasha scooted closer to her fire, her pearl and onyx bracelets clacking down her wrist as she drew pointed circles in the air around her. Magic sizzled brightly before disappearing like fireflies, requests to the cosmos for a closer look. They returned with sizzling zaps, creating a picture in her starlit mind.

The surface answer was clear enough: baleful baren Queen Qadira wanted a bouncing babe to call her own. But the fire haze around the queen obscured the center of the picture, and Pasha had to throw sage thrice on the sparking blue fire to see Queen Qadira as a whole. At first, Pasha thought the obscurity was because Queen Qadira's witches and warlocks were protecting her. But Ursa usually made quick work of Cancer's concealing magic.

There was something more powerful, more tempting, more... chaotic blocking her way

An ephemeral light was blocking the string of magic she had thrown at the queen—a dark and sticky light that consumed as much as it gave off. Pasha focused her magic and sent pulse after pulse through the string. The green of her magic pooled against the strain. She absentmindedly chewed on the petrified wood of her beaded necklace, slipping into a trance as she pushed against the force. Then the gate shattered.

Her magic flowed through easily, swirling into a cosmic circle dotted with stars. The culprit became clear. Another celestial had already claimed Qadira. One who called himself Kakkab.

Which led to the next question: Why was this other presence the reason Pisces refused the beleaguered queen's request? It was evident enough the two would be at odds, but far worse djinn and humans both had born children after slaughtering thousands. General Bakr of Shihala had single-handedly slaughtered legions of Vespars and had nearly half a dozen bouncing babes already.

She pulled the strings of Ursa's finding magic, ever-present in her current state of servitude to the ancient bitty, and prodded that line more deeply.

It was prodding the star that she found something delectable: Pisces wanted the queen just as much as she wanted him—some unsettled debt for a slaughtered lower witch who played his strings. And the tastiest tidbit of all: Pisces eagerly hungered for the end of death which purportedly came from a constellation named Kakkab.

What was more delicious than deceit and deception tearing the powerful apart? The whole coming together was an absolute delight.

All she had to do was to tell Pisces his bounty had been answered and she would fulfill the queen's request and Pisces' bounty, allowing her to collect both rewards. Pasha could then use the boon she'd gain from the Celestial of Life to barter her freedom from Ursa and sink into a life of cozy wealth subsidized by the queen's payout.

Things were looking up, and Pasha made sure to slay a toad in gratitude. Then, she sent a message informing El Anaaji that her request had been granted.

CHAPTER TWENTY-TWO

Dee

The chaos in King Malqum's burned bedchambers broke like shattered glass, filling Dee's mind with painful silence. The clang of daggers. The yells as Nazdael and Lahm—How could it be Lahm?—sparred. The splatter of blood as blades tore skin. And the tinkling of Nazdael's bells.

They all came to nothing.

Then, in the silence, Kakkab's voice, deep and quiet.

Will you risk a death now, Qa-di-ra?

Her heart dropped into her stomach like a comet and broke the silence. The cacophony of noise smashed into her, causing her to gasp.

"Dee!" Lahm's voice carried through the mayhem.

She snapped her eyes to his pale and haggard face. A brace wrapped around his stomach, and a bandage around his head. His left arm hung in a sling, and his foot, twisted in a grotesque angle, limped along in a muslin bandage. He barely managed to parry and dodge, the slim dagger in his hand no match for Nazdael's glittering silver and the magic it contained. He coughed in the drifting purple haze. Sweat marked his brow. Panic his eyes. But he was alive.

For now.

Kakkab's threat hung heavy in her mind as the star snickered in her ear with renewed vigor.

"Dee!" Lahm called again, Nazdael's blade slicing the skin of his bicep. He winced and flung himself back. "Help!"

His plea snapped her mind back to the present. Without a weapon that Kakkab refused to conjure and an arm that didn't work, knocking Nazdael off her balance was her best bet.

Qadira hurled herself at Nazdael's knees. The two tumbled to the floor, and Nazdael's blade pressed broadside into Qadira's useless arm, burning her flesh. She shrieked and tried to scramble away. Nazdael yanked her foot back with a scream, then rolled on top of Qadira and raised her blade. A heavy *smack* reverberated around the room, and Nazdael fell forward, grasping the back of her head. Blood trickled through her fingers.

Dee shot wide eyes at Lahm who stood behind her, breathing heavily. His hand curled around a thick piece of cobblestone, now dashed with red.

Nazdael slumped off Qadira. Her cries mingled with shrieks, and blood oozed heavily from her hairline.

"Come on," Lahm said, dropping the stone and reaching for her. "Let's get out of here."

Dee looked at his hand—tangible and real—still unable to believe he was there. She held her breath and raised her one good arm so she could grasp his hand, finding her feet for the first time since that morning.

Then, she hesitated. "What about Nazdael?"

"What about her?" Lahm's brows furrowed.

Dee glanced between her elder sister and Lahm, the star's threat whispering in her ear, though Kakkab was strangely silent.

Someone must die. But now Lahm lived.

Her stomach wrenched. She couldn't risk killing him. Not again. And now that he lived, she selfishly didn't want to die, either.

"We—" She dropped her voice to a whisper. "We have to finish her."

A strange look flitted across his eyes, orange and flashing, surprised and appalled. But wouldn't he have told her the same? She squeezed her hands together at her side, pinching the silk of her pants in her hands. Uncertainty squiggled inside her, making her nauseous.

"Lahm?"

He shook his head, pulling his hair and glancing at Nazdael. "I don't know."

Dee balked. "What do you mean, you don't know? Weren't you the one prepping for this day? Preparing strategies and getting ready for what needed to be done? Planning the fire and everything with Ba? And now that we're here—"

She held her breath, Hulon's words brushing the forefront of her mind.

"You weren't planning on me doing all the killing, were you?"

"Of course not," Lahm snapped, voice weary.

"Then, what?" She let go of his hand and pointed at Nazdael. "What exactly were you expecting would happen in the Allaedam *you* started? You made *me* start?"

His face fell, and her heart squeezed, shooting pain into her hands. She was surprised. Angry. Hurt. Relieved. And ultimately, helplessly confused.

Lahm grabbed his injured elbow and shuffled his feet. "I didn't mean to—to kill Ma like that."

"You?" She scoffed, then, surprised she had done so, snapped her jaw shut. "The strategist? The one Hulon thought most dangerous? The mind behind the shadow?"

"Shadow?" He raised his eyes, then dropped them once more. "It was an oversight. I had scheduled the Quwian placement before Ma got sick. I didn't think about how she would be weak and just above the explosion when it happened."

The flame Hulon had ignited inside her dwindled, an unsettling doubt taking its place. Nazdael groaned on the cold tile and clutched at her head, her ribs.

"I knew I wasn't ready for this." Lahm pressed knuckles into his eyes. "I thought I had time. Years. Decades even, to get ready. I'm not like you. I'm not so brave."

"Brave?" Dee's fists loosened. Her fingers widened. Then her arms. The explosion of emotions she felt burst out into furious tears. She rushed forward and hugged him.

"I'm so sorry about the window. About Chiba. About listening to everything Hulon said and thinking badly of you. I'm so sorry."

His one good arm wrapped around her back. "I saw him talking to you down in the courtyard near the fire, but what could he possibly have to say about me?"

Dee swallowed and pulled back so she could see her brother's jade eyes. "That you killed Ma on purpose and didn't tell me… that you might still be alive… that you—" She inhaled sharply and closed her mouth.

"That I betrayed you? Put you up to all of this?" he asked, gazing steadily at her. Blood dripped from a cut in his eyebrows, red contrasting the green of his irises.

She nodded and dropped her eyes to her slippers, heat inflaming her cheeks. It felt silly now, saying it aloud.

He tousled her hair and patted her shoulder. "It's okay Dee. You've been through Jahannam and back since I apparated from this place this morning."

"This morning," she sighed. Then she tilted her head. "What happened this morning? You came back and were about to tell me something when—when—" She buried her face in her hands.

"What I have to say doesn't matter anymore." He gave an uneasy glance toward Nazdael who had settled into quiet sobs, her body curved in the child's pose and hair strewn like a snake about her. "I came to tell you the news about Ma and that Todor had seen Nazdael spying on us in the courtyard."

"Todor?" Dee repeated slowly. "But why are you and Nazdael up here?"

He smiled. "I thought you might return, it being our home base and all."

She flushed.

"It's why I was hiding up here. After I fell, I nearly died. My ribs separated. The back of my head is fairly bashed in. I grabbed that bit of cobblestone I hit Nazdael with as the guards dragged me away and threw me in the infirmary, waiting for me to die. Everything went grey. Then black. I was ready for my life to slip away. And then it didn't. Light and thought returned, air found my lungs, and blood my veins. It was like a sconce had been lit inside my body, and I was back. Todor found me there. He bandaged me up and helped drag me out of there before anyone saw us. Then he brought me up here, tucked me away, and left to find a healing potion. Nazdael came up shortly after and made herself at home. At that point, I was just trying to hide in the dark so she didn't fill my lungs with her sour magic."

"A healing potion? But those were all confiscated and locked up the second the Allaedam was called. Not to mention they're rare."

"We know the rules." He shrugged. "I may be alive, but I'm not in good shape. I'd say barely breathing. A fight with anyone on my own right now would mean my death."

Dee pursed her lips before snapping her head up. "Does that mean you are dying?"

"I fell from five stories, Dee-Dee-Ra. I'm lucky I had enough energy and mental capacity to apparate up here, much less fight Nazdael with you. I should be dead." He tilted his head toward Nazdael, a sick look twitching across his lips.

Dee's heart picked up, implications stabbing at her like a knife.

That's right, little queen. You see it now, don't you?

Dee looked at Nazdael, pathetic in a weeping, bleeding heap. Harmless. Defeated. She would give in. Agree to leave. But then, who would die?

Qadira swept her gaze up to her brother. The words that came out of her mouth tasted like bitter sumac. "We must finish her, Lahm. It's the only way."

He shoved a hand in his pocket and narrowed his eyes with a sharpness that hadn't been there before. "I don't think so, Dee. I think I was wrong."

She scoffed, heat burbling in her chest. "You're joking, right? After everything we've been through. No, there's no way. You said that you wanted to rule with me. You and I. Not you and I and Nazdael.

Lahm pursed his lips. "If we can change the rules for you and me, we can change them for everyone."

"Hulon would never agree. You're wasting your time." Dee's stomach snarled into a terrible knot.

"Maybe he would," Lahm said, though doubt crossed his face. He turned from her and walked to the other side of the room, glancing out the narrow window so darkness hid only half his face. "Nazdael was about to agree before she went crazy. What was she saying to you about stars and deals?"

Yes. What was she saying, again? Something about the deal you're going to make with me? Or was it that you already made one and use my power when you want to kill?

"It's complicated..." she began, but worry itched in her chest.

Don't want to tell him about your new bestie? I'm hurt. He'd only think you mad or deranged. There are far worse things. Though if you killed him and ascended as queen, he wouldn't have any thoughts to think. Then you could crack my little cage under your heel and be done with me. There would be no blackness darkening your soul any longer. I've helped save you from death already, the least I could do is save you this embarrassment, too.

Lahm narrowed his eyes, her silence too long. "Well?" He dropped his chin and looked up at her, skepticism written in every wrinkle of his face.

Dee clenched her teeth. Now wasn't the time to tell him about Kakkab. Not when she needed him to trust her so she could keep him alive. She'd explain everything once he was safe.

"It doesn't matter," Dee said through clenched teeth. "She's a witch who wants me dead. She wants you dead, too. There's only one way out of this."

Lahm's brows shot together and then eased out, his lips falling into a frown. "What are you saying? Look at her." He stretched a hand out toward Nazdael's sniveling heap. "It would be cold-blooded murder."

"So?" Qadira snapped. "Isn't that the whole point of this? To prove who can rule by taking care of the competition no matter what?"

Hurt twisted across Lahm's face. "Is that how you see me? Competition?"

"Of course not," Dee snipped, heart warping with the crinkle in his brows. "I don't trust that she won't try and kill us after we make a deal with her. I don't trust... anyone. Anyone but Vawk and you." Dee reached forward and squeezed his hand, a whirlwind billowing inside her and breathing out her lips. "I need you to live."

"And I need you to be Dee-Dee-Ra. Not some ruthless queen who kills her siblings."

A coldness swept over her, filling in the hollowness left by Chiba's death. She didn't want to kill. To be seen as powerful and marked as a target or be a ruthless queen. But survival left little room for kindness.

Qadira tilted her chin up and looked at Lahm. "It is what I was born to do!"

"You don't believe that do you?" he asked, voice softer than Nazdael's sniffling, so she had to lean in and listen.

Qadira looked at their intertwined fingers, her shining confidence still weak around Lahm. "Please," she mouthed, beseeching Kakkab. "Please don't make me do this."

You know the price.

"Take me, instead."

And disappear into the dirt? That was your threat, wasn't it? I take threats very seriously. But if you'd like to end your own life...

Qadira shuttered, self-preservation balking at the thought. She wasn't brave. Not like Lahm thought. At least, not yet. But if she could survive long enough... if she could be the cold person she needed to be and make it to the end, she'd have a chance to show him she was still the sister he believed her to be.

Let me out, little girl. I will kill the bewitched one and spare you and your brother.

She blanched, glancing between Lahm, who stared desolately at the floor, and where her right earring hung, warm against her cheek. "No." Her mouthing changed to a husky whisper "I can't trust you around Lahm. All you do is cause unwanted death. I will... kill her myself."

As you wish. Though it may be hard when you don't mean it.

She bared her teeth and clenched her one free hand, trying to prove him wrong. But he was right. No weapon appeared. Even when Lahm's life was on the line and the only answer was clear, she couldn't find the heart to murder. To do what it took to save what she cared most for. To be queen. Because that's what royalty did, wasn't it? Give of themselves to save their people?

I grow bored and lethargic without my supper. Perhaps another little fall for your brother will satisfy my needs?

She threw down Lahm's hand and turned her back to him, snarling as she summoned a heavy morning star with obsidian caps on each of its points that came to rest gently in her palm. The rough wood chaffed her fingers, evoking drops of angry blood as she tightened her grip.

"Let's end this."

FIFTH CULLING

A Formal Allaedam Declaration

By the grace and providence of the Celestial Bahamut on the 35th day of the Seventh Moon's One-Thousandth Shadow Pass, in the time of the Fifteenth Allaedam to secure the throne of Ahmar, a culling eliminated the weak and chaotic. During the Allaedam, the Eighth Heir of the True Nine who have claim to the throne of Ahmar killed the Fourth True Heir by brutal bludgeoning with an archaic, obsidian morning star. Death confirmed by blood fire through the mangled heart, the battered remains beyond recognition.

The official record of True Heirs to the Ahmaran throne reads as:

First True Heir, Shutor - Honorably killed by the Third Heir for his country

Second True Heir, Talcum - Honorably killed by the Third Heir for his country

Third True Heir, Hulon - Living at 25 years old

Fourth True Heir, Nazdael - Honorably killed by the Eighth Heir for her country

Fifth True Heir, Bruella - Honorably killed by the Eighth Heir for her country

Sixth True Heir, Icha - Honorably killed by the Eighth Heir for her country

Seventh True Heir, Lahmdan - Honorably killed by the Eighth Heir for her country

Eighth True Heir, Qadira - Living at 13 years old

Ninth and final True Heir, Chiba - Honorably killed by the Eighth Heir for her country

No other deaths are yet recorded as the country awaits the victor of the Allaedam, but with the Bahamut as Ahmar's witness, only one heir can rule.

CHAPTER TWENTY-THREE

Ursa Major

Ursa had not been three mortal months into her deliberations when Kakkab's temper shattered the balance in the heavens. A shock wave knocked a few minor stars off course and caused a tidal wave of discontent that reached her expanse.

Her aura flared. The vindictive hothead couldn't leave things be. She said she would handle it. She always did. She was the Grand Decider. She was the Finder. She knew all things, and nothing, not even scalding Cancer, could hide from her. Yet Kakkab was dumb enough to chase The Goose, that little brat of a mischief star, to his doom.

Ursa swooped her aura up and, pulling on the powers of Aquarius, shot across the universes, a streak of silver across the purpling black. When she arrived in The Goose's home solar system, she sucked in tight.

Empty. His planets wandered around nothing, left to a spacial drift they may never recover from. Not to mention the centuries of ice and darkness with no star to warm and guide them.

Irresponsible. Foolish. Neglectful of divine command. But The Goose was not solely to blame.

Next, she shot to Kakkab and found as she suspected. The burning ball of pure temper had abandoned his system as well. Not just his aura, but his entire being, which made his intentions clear. He was out to destroy.

With a great seizing fire in her belly, Ursa channeled her magic and shot strings in a splay of rainbow light across the darkness, searching for the two fools who were determined to make this millennium unpleasant.

Their magic pulsed far away, on a tiny planet in the middle of nothing important. She groaned internally and shot over, temper nearly as hot as theirs must be. But what she found stopped her in her tracks.

With a degree of thought, she condensed and sunk onto Qaf. Her light transferred its form into a room where a red djinn knelt on both knees, hands clasped to the stars. In front of him, still battling in angry swirls of light and matter, were the very stars she looked for. A seal-skinned box with red shells stood open before him, along with a glass globe that hummed and a black pyramid that consumed light and stank of evil.

"Mortal," she quipped, her voice as smooth as the milky way. Her corporeal form consisted of warm brown skin, starlit white hair, and full lips she loved to smack.

The djinn snapped his head toward her, then fell back. "Demon!"

"Hardly," she smiled. "More like savior, today. Tell me, why do you beseech such angry stars."

"Because I am angry."

She raised a thin brow—an action she frequently wished she could perform as an aura. "And what do you hope to accomplish with your anger and the magic of chaos and death?"

"Chaos and death."

Her other brow raised. "At least you are aware of your stupidity. If I may ask, how are you planning to wrangle these two powerful beings? Even now, when you use powerful artifacts you do not understand to call on their magic as a devout, they do not listen."

The red djinn's face fell. He covered it with shaking hands. "My daughter has been trapped by a terrible king. She dies slowly every day as he whores about and defiles her. Please—Please, help me."

She smiled. "Only because it suits me."

Ursa snapped her fingers and the two swirling veils of mist pulled apart, their little globules of light still reaching to strangle each other. "Quickly now, give me something to put them in."

The djinn scooped up two handfuls of sand and cast yellow fire through the grains. Two little crystal droplets formed in each, and Ursa smiled, satisfied. They were the perfect receptacles for the misbehaved. Tiny and cramped and strong enough to keep them in, with a little help of course.

She snapped her fingers again, and Kakkab's dark light zipped into one, Anser's weak light to the other. Then, because she was all about sensibility, she fashioned the droplets into a matching pair of earrings.

The father watched, eyes wide, as the two droplets floated up to her eye level.

"I've decided on my sentences early, you starry little brats." She clinked her nail against each crystal. "Kakkab, for your foolishness, I'm trapping you with Anser until you learn not to let fools goad you. Because of your temper and because I'm fed up, you won't be able to leave your cage until you save someone's life and convince them to let you out. As the constellation of all things death, I'm sure mortals will jump at the idea of letting you out. We all know they're creatures of their word." She smirked.

"And Anser—" Ursa sniffed as she said his name, irritated she had to speak to such a lowly star. How did such a pathetic Celestial ever come to rule a constellation in the first place? "You dumb little Goose, you are to remain in exile until you create order instead of destroying it. Then, you must do the same as Kakkab and beg whatever mortal you befall to let you out. A feat indeed knowing your true nature and how much Kakkab despises when you speak."

"And don't try any funny business again, you twits. If one of you finds your freedom without the other, you may not intercede in the punishment of the other in any way. Once free, however, you both shall consider the other one absolved, having paid for their crimes with this fun little experiment. Oh—" She lifted the pair of earrings and winked. "—and no magic for yourselves. If you want something done, you'll have to beg it from a mortal. A good punishment for two buffoons with too much pride."

Ursa nodded with satisfaction and met the djinn's lingering gaze. His mouth hung open, hands resting on each side of the swirling pyramid of darkness. He swallowed so hard, the bulge in his throat bobbed.

"Make sure they stay together." Ursa smiled.

The djinn father nodded furiously.

"Good. They won't be able to torture each otherwise, and that's half the punishment. And good luck to you and your daughter, though you did not choose to call on that Celestial." She laughed. "You mortals make the strangest choices, always focusing on the dark when there's so much light."

Satisfied, she left her lovely mortal frame and shot back to the heavens.

CHAPTER TWENTY-FOUR

She raised the morning star from the crumpled body of her sister and readjusted her grip on the sticky handle. With a final putrid breath, she let it fall one last time. The spikes landed with a squishy crunch.

Her breaths fell heavy. Her good arm shook with exhaustion and her bad with pain. She shuttered and wiped her blood-splattered cheeks on her shoulder. Kakkab's cruel laughter had long ago faded into background noise. Something that simply was.

Nazdael's glittering cloud had thinned with every heavy-handed blow, clearing the room except for a layer of sparkles that clung to the splatters of Nazdael's blood, coating her like a new skin.

She turned, looking for Lahmdan. But the room was empty.

He was gone. And she felt nothing.

Well done, glittering queen. The world will see your glister and fear.

She dropped the morning star and walked to the window to look down upon the courtyard. The guards had managed to reduce the flames of her bedchambers to irritated embers. A glowing tomb for little Chiba.

There were only the three of them left now, her and Lahmdan and Hulon. The Allaedam would end soon. The people would have their ruler.

A small part of her wanted to sink to her knees, curl up into a ball, and sob her eyes out. But the bigger part of her knew that it was impossible. There wasn't a single tear left to cry. Not a bit of her heart that hadn't been bludgeoned, like her sister's body.

Though in the center, protected by viscera and muscle and her one last hope, was a pearl the shape of Lahmdan.

She closed her eyes and apparated freely through where Nazdael's firewalls had blocked her before. She landed in the hidden hallways outside the throne room and walked with steady steps out through the curtain she had fallen through before. All signs of Icha had been wiped away, leaving a clean canvas of white and blue marble for her bloody footprints. She headed out of the large wooden doors and took off her shoes, sick of the stick and slip.

Once free of the throne room's protective layers, she thought of Vawk and apparated to his side. He paced his bedchambers, the air thick and acrid so close they were to hers.

"*Ya lawhy!*" he gasped, falling backward into a tall set of brocade curtains. He fought the fabric as if it were a drakonte, finally extricating himself in a huff. "Don't do that!"

She raised her gaze to his, the edges of her vision blurry.

"Mercy!" His face dropped. "Come, come, my princess. Let me clean you up." He shooed her toward a tiny room meant for washing.

She pushed his outstretched hand away. "I don't have time."

"And why not?" he asked with a *harrumph*. "I don't see Hulon around unless you're hiding him in the puff of your pants. He's the only one we have to worry about now, isn't he? I heard the bonehorns announce the witch's culling. And Bruella is safely poised to flee the palace as soon as the Allaedam's restrictions are lifted. We are well on our way to ruling Ahmar, little queen."

She shook her head and slapped his reaching hand away. "Lahmdan lives."

Vawk sputtered and his chin flapped up and down. "How?"

She shrugged, aching and cold. "Does it matter?"

He pursed his lips, eyes scanning her bruised and bloodied body. "What are you going to do?"

"Whatever I have to to keep him alive."

"But Qadira—"

"What?" She turned on him, a fire flickering in her eyes that she thought was dead.

He raised his hands and eased back from her. "You know the rules... Only one can rule the great nation of Ahmar."

"Lahm doesn't think so."

"Whether your twin thinks so or not, the rules are written," Vawk said. "Only one can live. Only one can rule. One of you will have to die to keep Ahmar from a terrible war that will split it apart and leave it weak to our enemies."

His words *cracked* in her brain, so similar to Kakkab's. To her own as she bludgeoned her cowering sister while she huddled helplessly on the floor. Dee's eye twitched, and a shudder traveled from her spine up her neck, rattling her thoughts.

"If one must die, let it be me. I've already given my soul so Lahm won't have to give his. What's my body, too?"

"Qadira!"

"*What*?" she snapped again, but the look of hurt betrayal on his face smothered the stirring fire. "I don't know what you want from me. I don't even know who I am anymore. I don't know who to be. All I know is that I'm nothing without Lahm. He's the most important thing to me. He is my good."

Vawk's lips curled. "I see."

She sighed and covered her face with her one working hand. Red and white, blood and glitter. The feel of splintered wood. Kakkab's words in her mind once again. She dropped her arm.

Crack.

"I'm sorry Vawk." She ground her teeth together and forced her hand to unclench. "But I trust Lahm. And if we can't find a way to rule together, I don't want to rule at all. Your and my deaths will be in honor of our country, and you will be granted eternal salvation for your loyalty."

Her eternal future was in the fires of Jahannam. It was all the better he couldn't follow.

Vawk's mouth stayed shut, though his eyes spoke volumes, his black irises winking with brackish yellow and baleful blue. He spitefully feared as much as he hoped.

She understood that. The swirl of opposites in a single mind. But hers were different. Love for Lahmdan. Disgust for herself. Hatred for the being still cackling in her ear. How else could she bash Nazdael's head in with a morning star and splatter brain across the floor? She'd throw the earring down a well, except she didn't trust Kakkab would stay there. He'd find a new soul to haunt soon enough, then hunt Lahmdan down, bent on retribution for her not releasing him. She also needed the belligerent being. At least, she did for now. Though she'd never admit it out loud, Kakkab forced her to ignore her fears and do what needed to get done.

"What is your plan, princess?" Vawk finally whispered.

"To find Hulon and kill him." The words rolled easily off her tongue, like rote facts about the Ahmaran climate she had memorized as a child "Then to find Lahmdan and explain."

"As you wish." He bobbed his head, eyes not meeting hers. "What do you require of me?"

"To let happen what will."

Silence.

His shoulders hunched, making him smaller. He whispered once more, "As you wish."

CHAPTER TWENTY-FIVE

The Courtesan

THE COURTESAN FINGERED THE earrings her father had sent, heart pounding. King Malqum's servant had come, requesting her presence in His Majesty's chambers. It was now or never. *Now or never.* Or later, perhaps, if she backed down like she had so many times before. But fear was unsustainable. Every night she waited to use the power her father had sent, breath heavy and heart hurting, the more her soul fractured into tinier and tinier pieces.

It had to be tonight.

That's right, mortal, the deep voice of Death whispered in her ear. *Find your courage and draw on my magic to kill the king. You will be saved and my debt repaid. Then you can release me.*

She nodded to the servant and wrapped her silk robes around her otherwise naked body, freshly bathed and scented like the taluli that graced the palace walls. The scent was overwhelmingly floral, like a dozen bouquets from every continent in Qaf had been ground up together. The only thing in Qaf she hated more was the king.

I disagree, on principle, another voice spoke up, this one Misfortune. *Killing the king will only cause an uprising. You will be hunted and killed, if you escape at all. Then war will stir in the country and hundreds of thousands of lives could be lost. Is that something you want on your conscience?*

She followed the servant, quiet footsteps echoing in spacious halls.

The queen was out to banquet, she had been told, schmoozing other princesses in a sort of queenly regale of debauchery, giving the king plenty of time to debauch himself.

It was only a few short degrees until the courtesan arrived at the king's bedchambers on the fifth story, a quiet set of rooms tucked out of the way with views of the courtyard. During the entire clandestine stroll of the palace, the stars bickered in her ear. They did every time.

Killing the king is what she deserves.

And what does the nation deserve?

The nation does not belong to her, only her life does.

One for the many seems a fair sacrifice to me.

Since when do you want order?

Since when don't you want death?

She took a deep breath and entered the room. King Malqum's bloodservant grabbed the back of her robes and pulled them from her naked shoulders. The soft fabric fell to the floor, leaving her exposed and cold, vulnerable to the whims of the capricious king.

King Malqum reposed on his bed, creamy sheets hiding his excitement from the dim djinn-fire lamps. He had trimmed his beard so it came to a sharp point just below his neck and had oiled his purple abs and pecs so they shined. His chest was hairless, his smile slack. He turned to make a spot for her in the pillows next to him, allowing her time to suppress her exuberant revulsion. She bowed to the king when he turned back and brushed a finger over the earring.

Ask, that's all you need do, mortal. Ask and I will grant what you deserve. Salvation from this terrible king, Death said.

She wanted salvation. She wanted to ask. The king's fate was her punishment to decide, her father had said so. Her decision and no one else's. She bit her lip. Shuffled her feet. Raised her gaze to meet the king's green eyes glowing red with the embers of lustful heat.

Sensing her hesitation, King Malqum rose from the bed and cupped her face in his hands. She pressed her hands against his shaved chest, her red skin wrong against the soft purple, like lavender cut to bleed.

"What troubles my princess?"

She looked away.

"You turn from your king?"

She winced and bit her lip, refusing to look at him lest the pink of uncertainty color her normally yellow eyes. She needed to do it. To whisper her desire for death upon the king.

But he is a king, Misfortune countered, *however despicable he may be. Do you wish to plunge a nation into chaos for your gain? Is the king's head worth eternal damnation?*

The courtesan curled her toes, chest aching with her dwindling courage. She didn't want to burn for eternity, she just wanted to be free.

"My love," the king prodded gently, then tilted her chin up so her gaze would drift to his. "Such weight rests upon your mind. Let us remove your earrings and free you of a burden. I want you truly naked when you stand before me."

He reached for the crystal globe in her left ear.

Don't let him take it, Death hissed.

"Wait," she whispered, harsher than she meant.

The king furrowed his brow and pulled back. "You tell me what to do?"

"No, I—" she fumbled, her prowess in speaking long withered away after the years of solitude she had been forced to endure. Her silence was what he liked best about her.

King Malqum slipped a crooked finger under the loop and pulled it from her ear.

That wasn't good.

She scrunched her toes against the cold floor and tried to keep her eyes from widening.

The king now has Misfortune, and you know what his wish for the king was. He will destroy you now if we don't do it first.

The courtesan gasped before she could stop herself. She flinched, fearful the king heard, but he continued to gaze, eyes crimson as ever, unaware of the whispers in her ear.

"I excite you, my darling?" the king asked, licking her ear. He hooked the earring over his thumb, so his fingers were free to caress her.

She cringed but forced herself still.

Do it. Now. Strengthen yourself with my magic and ask for his death. Then, when he's dead, release me, and I will protect you from the consequences.

A shiver raced down the courtesan's spine, though it was hard to tell if they came from the terrible voice or the king's tongue licking down her neck. She bit her lip and shook her head. How badly she wanted to free the beast and how fearful she was to do so. Then the king's hand found its way to her chest and squeezed.

"How?" she blurted, eyes cinched tight.

King Malqum's hand stopped moving. "Excuse me?"

Her heart shot into her throat, making it hard to speak. She thought carefully, searching for a way out of her outburst. "I wish to release you, my King, this very evening, but I don't know how. Please, tell me."

He chuckled softly, an unsettling mix that blended with the snickers in her ear. "I shall do the work, my love. Simply be the receptacle of my satisfaction."

She shivered.

After the king passes, shatter the glass that binds me, and I shall be free.

The courtesan trembled again, then reached up and pulled the earring from her ear. She thought of the king's death, of sheets wrapping around his neck, of him screaming. The earring glowed warmer in her hands.

Do it. Do it quickly. Now. The being's pleas matched the pound of her heart.

She thought again of the king's demise like she had so many times before but nothing happened. Nothing ever did. Why? Why was she so weak? She wasted her father's gift. And this time, she would die.

King Malqum breathed heavily against her neck, pawing, licking, and calling her sweet names that made her retch.

And still, she held the earring.

Channel me and feel my magic, The voice hissed. *Give me this death, and let me be free.*

The courtesan sealed her eyes tighter, muscles tense, the heat of tears threatening the corners of her eyes. She hated her life. She wanted out. Maybe it didn't matter which way it went. Whether she killed the king or he killed her, either way, the nightmare would end.

You have woken me yet refuse to accept my aid. You will die when you could be saved. Death's voice sounded edgy, pleading.

King Malqum bit her ear hard enough, she winced. His hands moved across her chest and up, then slowly slid around her neck. Her eyes widened. His grip tightened. Tighter and tighter.

Kill him, Death pleaded. *Kill the king!*

And faintly, from where the king still held Chaos in his fingers, was the whisper, *Kill her, kill her, she can never be queen.*

"No!" She screamed and raised her clenched fist. "No more!"

Her djinn fire burst forth from her fingers, an inferno of rage manifesting in scalding flames of yellow as high as the ceiling.

The king yelled and drew back towards the bed and away from the doorway. She dove and grabbed his wrist before he could apparate away from her.

"Witch," he scrambled to get away, clawing at her hands as the earring jingled in his hands.

The power of the stars channeled through her this time, fueled by her rage at being something to so many but never herself. But, like her temper, the magic was too much for her to control. The flames poured in blasts of boiling heat. Her skin began to shred with heat and light, the yellow of her djinn fire the same as her father's.

The king's beard caught alight, his purple skin reddening to a shade she had missed from home. She let him go and ran for the exit, but he caught her from behind and fell upon her.

"You little *eahira!*" the king screamed.

The flesh on his fingers melted where they touched her, but she couldn't escape. His weight was upon her body, his hate upon her soul.

She spat in his face. He snarled, his lips falling off his face and onto where they had kissed her neck. She screamed. He melted. But it was too late.

The bedchambers were consumed within a single degree.

CHAPTER TWENTY-SIX

QADIRA

QADIRA STEPPED OUT OF Vawk's chambers and thought of Hulon. Of his sneering face. His oily lies. How accurate he had been when he called her a shadow, though, at the time, she had not been. She was in the becoming now. A shade of death that would cover his last moments. Or hers.

There could be only one.

She closed her eyes and apparated to her only living brother, reappearing on the coarse, grey stone that made up the palace parapets. Wind whipped her braid, snapping it so the remnants of sparkle jumped off and disappeared in the moonlight. Snaps of light in an otherwise dark light.

Hulon stood at the edge of the castle wall, hands folded neatly behind his back and facing the view. Ahmar glittered and winked all around them, watching and waiting for one of them to prove their loyalty to the people. To give up their own family for the hungry masses.

"Sister."

"Brother."

"You took care of the witch, did you?"

"Her fire still burns in my nostrils." Qadira took a step closer, strands of black hair tousling across her vision. "Her blood still drips from my hands."

"A bit graphic for my tastes, but I won't complain." He turned, a glistening smile between parted lips. "You did me a favor there, little shadow. I can only imagine the fight she put up."

Qadira's stomach curdled. Bits of Nazdael flashed in her mind. Begging screams. Bloodied fingers. Reaching. Clawing. Eyes doused in fearful black.

Crack.

"Tooth for tooth. Fire for fire. She made her bed when she was born, as did you and I."

"Wise words, little Qadira. Wiser than I thought you capable."

He turned to face her fully, his usual scimitar nowhere in sight. Instead, an Urumi whip snapped in his hand, eight curling blades of sharp, glinting metal that extended the length of his from a thick, leather handle. Any brush of the metal would sear her djinn skin and any knick of the edge would tear at her skin. A warbling, bendy sound cut the air every time he moved his wrist, and eight reflections of herself peered back at her, each with eyes of a different color.

"You know I must end you," he said, voice calm as a mother's shoosh.

"It will be what it is."

"Indeed." Hulon stepped towards her and flicked the Urumi out to the side. The *twang* of metal skipped across the stone, echoing in the whirlwind around her. "I have a simple request of you."

"And why would I do anything for you?" She raised her chin defiantly, grateful the roar of wind drove away the sounds of the evil in her ear.

"Because I will make death swift and merciful."

"I'd rather die from a thousand stab wounds than do a favor for you."

He smirked, cruel and knowing. "I didn't mean a swift end for you. I must make an example out of your death. What a conundrum you've left the people. The slayer of witches and five-year-olds alike."

Crack.

She blinked a few times to clear her jumbled thoughts, then sought the root of his threat. "If not my death, then whose?"

"Why, Lahmdan's of course."

Crack.

"Ah." He smiled. "There it is."

She clenched her trembling jaw and looked away.

"I thought he was alive, despite the bonehorns' declaration. You see, I caught his Todor out in the hallways, scrambling for a potion, the little cheat. After a bit of torture, he told me he had almost died with Lahm, ribs cracked and head panging. He waited for death, but, instead, strength returned to his limbs and clarity to his mind. He picked himself up from the floor of Lahmdan's bedchambers and went to bring him aid. He found him, hid him somewhere in the palace, and told him to be quiet. He was blathering on about a morning star and blood, viscera, and a crazy witch, you see. Though I'm not sure I know who that last one referred to. Do you?"

Crack.

"Of course, he refused to tell me where Lahmdan hid, and I couldn't let him live if he was going to play dirty. But you know how it is." Hulon rolled his shoulder and revealed a wince.

His chest wound? Dee made a note somewhere in the tumbling anger of her mind.

Hulon walked around her, the sound of his steps a steady base to the warp of metal across stone. Any one of the blades could both eviscerate and scald her flesh with the tiniest knick. The air shimmered around them. The strips of steel scattered moonlight across the taluli that bloomed freely between the merlons of the rampart, a testament to what was to come.

He spun to face her and snapped the whips. "Tell me where he's hiding, and I'll let him pass to judgment as mercifully as I am able."

"Impossible with your cruel tongue," she spat. "I ought to cut it out."

Hulon laughed and pressed a palm to his chest. Thick leather bracers protected his forearms against the sting of his metal whips. "That's quite a threat from a little thing like you."

"Fight me."

Hulon cut off his laughter. "How? Your shoulder is useless, and you don't have a weapon."

"You're almost as wounded as I, though you try to hide it. And you're wrong about the weapon."

She rushed towards him, raising her fist. She clenched tight and let her anger strike.

Her fist landed.

He gasped and stepped back, eyes wide. The blades of his Urumi shivered off to the side, stray tips of metal catching bits of her skin, leaving tiny cuts and burns.

Then he fell back against the crennel.

And laughed.

Laughed and laughed. Hard and in his belly.

He pushed her back, so she stumbled.

Qadira looked down. Her hand was empty. Humiliation burbled in her cheeks and stung her ears. "Kakkab!"

Mortal?

"Why?"

You know the rules, child. I cannot make you something you are not any more than you apparently can. And you came so far.

Hulon snapped his whip to the side with a jangle of metal ends. "Who are you talking to?'

"All the times before—" Qadira seethed, chest tightening so she could hardly breathe, hardly able to speak the terrible words. "I wanted to kill."

You did.

"Why is this different?"

Because you are thinking of your elder brother right now. No matter how hard I tried, you are too weak to want to slay a mortal. A sibling. Every time a weapon has shown up, you've only wanted to kill me.

She snapped her head to the right. Her hair whipped and bit at her skin. "You goaded me on purpose!"

I did. Though it's your anger that fuels me. I only require death when your djinn fire runs too hot.

"Enough," Hulon cried, rattling his whip. "You are mad."

Her neck creaked as she turned to look at him. "No, I'm not. Not yet."

She leaped at him, summoning the star's strength into her arm and a thin line of shining thread to her hands, boiling with a desire to kill the immortal being. She landed against Hulon's chest and swung around, wrapping the string around his neck. The thread pulsed beneath her fingers and against his skin as if drinking Hulon up.

He screamed, one hand fumbling at the string and the other cracking the Urumi.

Pain and fire sliced through her ear, her eyebrow, in multiple flays along her arms. The thin blades made easy work of her puffed pants, tearing them open and staining them red. She screamed but held tight through the fiery assault. With every scream, she summoned more of Kakkab's magic. Her arm surged with strength, the earring with heat. The thread nicked at Hulon's skin, slowly making progress through his sweating flesh and her fingers, alike.

Blade after blade of his Urumi whip ate at her skin while her string stripped away his.

Tighter. Tighter.

She complied.

Harder. Harder.

She did.

As blood filled her vision. As her muscles begged for mercy, her bones for relief.

Hulon threw her off, and she slammed hard into the stony crennel. White spots shot across her vision, stars her mind. Hulon lunged. She rolled just in time. The Urumi swished past her in streams of rainbow light.

Pathetic. Weak. A shadow. A clutz.

Rage blinded her. She shot through the whipping metal blades and shoved Hulon back against the stone. His back bent over the sides, so the glittering lake caught the specks of their reflection below. She jumped on top of his chest, digging her elbow into his wound. Hot stickiness and the bitterness of djinn fire coated her arm. He snarled and screamed, trying to push her off, but she had the strength of a star. She clung tightly with her knees and pressed the cord against his throat. Power coursed from her earring, into her shoulder, and glowed brightly in the string she began to wrap around his neck, circle after circle like a necklace mortals wear.

Hulon choked and gagged. The Urumi dropped from his hand. In a last-ditch effort, he kicked himself off the parapet and tumbled on top of her. His always-green eyes now shone black and the sneer on his face held no triumph. Only hate. He slipped his fingers around her neck and squeezed.

Murderess. Killer. Fiend.

Her vision blurred. She squeezed tighter. So did he.

Qadira choked and sputtered, one thought bursting in her mind. Maybe they'd both end each other here, and Lahmdan would be free to ascend the throne without a drop of blood on his hands. Then he, not she, could remain good for Ahmar.

The thought built inside her, pouring her strength into that of the star. Her fingers closed in. Recognition skirted across Hulon's face. The same as hers only tinted with rage. His nails dug into her skin, expending the last of their energy so she would suffer for what she had done.

Then it ended. Everything in a snap of starlight.

Queen.

The string flashed bright white and inhaled all that was left of Hulon's life. She unwound her fingers and scurried back, dropping the thread. Its silky end raised from the ground, white marred with red, dark stained with light, and flicked toward her like an arrow. She screamed and cowered, falling to her knees. It flew past her nose and into the earring where Kakkab greedily drank it up.

What had happened?

She shoved Hulon off of her and gasped.

Hulon lay dead. Not from her string, but from a scimitar speared straight through his back.

SIXTH CULLING
A Formal Allaedam Declaration

By the grace and providence of the Celestial Bahamut on the thirty-fifth day of the Seventh Moon's One-Thousandth Shadow Pass, in the time of the Fifteenth Allaedam to secure the throne of Ahmar, a culling eliminated the weak and chaotic. During the Allaedam, the Eighth Heir of the True Nine who have claim to the throne of Ahmar killed the Third Heir with an Ahmaran gem-bladed scimitar, honorably for her country. The divine nation of Ahmar now awaits the ascendancy.

The official record of True Heirs to the Ahmaran throne reads as:
First True Heir, Shutor - Honorably killed by the Third Heir for his country
Second True Heir, Talcum - Honorably killed by the Third Heir for his country
Third True Heir, Hulon - Honorably killed by the Eight Heir for her country
Fourth True Heir, Nazdael - Honorably killed by the Eighth Heir for her country
Fifth True Heir, Bruella - Honorably killed by the Eighth Heir for her country
Sixth True Heir, Icha - Honorably killed by the Eighth Heir for her country
Seventh True Heir, Lahmdan - Honorably killed by the Eighth Heir for her country
Eighth True Heir, Qadira - Living at thirteen years old
Ninth and final True Heir, Chiba - Honorably killed by the Eighth Heir for her country

Only one True Heir remains. Long live Queen Qadira.

CHAPTER TWENTY-SEVEN

PISCES

THE ANSWER TO HIS bounty from the little Witch of Eternal Finding had interrupted Pisces' century-long sojourn into thought. It happened every time. He'd be a decade or two into his meditation when some insignificant, yowling mortal would come to pester him. He left his magic paths open for most just so he wouldn't be bothered.

It was always the few who shouldn't create life that seemed most insistent on doing so. He had tried to ignore them but soon found that peace came quicker if he spent the seconds and degrees required and just dealt with them.

That was how he learned that his immortal enemy lay helpless in an earring on Qaf, a tiny world attached to a tiny planet fourteen lightyears away. All it took to acquire him was a meeting with a mortal.

He rumbled to life and spun his aura to get the solar flares out, stretched a final time, and snapped his thoughts shorter to work on mortal time.

Kakkab, known to some as Taurus, had disappeared nearly two centuries before. Life had begun to proffer more in his absence and given Pisces an idea. Of course, Ursa urged caution and balance in all things, but if she ever had the chance to destroy Cancer, her deceiving opposite, he was certain she would use it to crush her. And who would dare stop him, anyway? No one in the cosmos would be foolish enough to destroy the magic of life. They'd stop all progression and sentence themselves to a slow, stagnate, and purposeless existence before cold death took them one by one.

A string of light cast towards him through the dark and hooked itself into his magic. The With of Eternal Finding had arranged the meeting and beseeched him to attend. He granted her request and shot toward Qaf in a rainbow comet of cosmic light.

Normally, he'd have mortals attend to him and not the other way around, but there was no way he would deign to let a murderous queen into his life-giving aura. The stain of such a dirty soul on his pure white would be irreversible.

Instead, he chose the slightly less abhorrent option and called on Aquarius's summoning magic to travel to the tiny planet. There, he forced his aura into the form of a djinn, a squashy suit of carbon and water that walked around on things called feet. He picked a coating for his body the color of the deep night sky and cast his constellation across it in warm, glowing dots of blue and yellow. Swirling vortexes showed through his seeing eyes, a glimpse into his true aura and as deep as time.

He appeared inside the queen's palace, their puny firewalls shivering in his presence, like stardust in a black hole. It took a moment to remember how this body worked, it having been several millennia since he last attempted a meeting in a cage of carbon.

Once he sorted out the strings to pull to get his appendages to move and called upon the magic of Pleiades for the knowledge of the language needed on this planet, he marched inside, directed by wide-eyed djinn who didn't know what to do with themselves. It wasn't until he reached a large set of doors—ridiculous contraptions made of a mixture of cellulose and lignin that only kept out the weakest of those with perishable bodies—he realized his mistake. He had made himself twice the size of the other djinn. He looked down, then up again at the puny little bodies of those around him. He also seemed to lack the garments they wore over their shoulders and draped across their midsections. Pisces pursed his djinn lips. Then shrugged. His body was glorious.

The queen stood in the center of a room with a crystal dome that looked to the heavens. Respectable. Maybe this mortal knew the importance of this meeting after all.

"Pisces," the slip of a woman spoke, dipping her head. "It is an honor to meet with the mighty Star of Life."

"Let's skip the superfluous emanation of sound, mortal. I do not wish to breathe in your recycled carbon dioxide."

Her eyes burned green like copper sulfate, then yellowed. "Very well. I want a baby. You refuse to grant me one. I wish to sway your mind for the good of Ahmar and my people, whom I've served faithfully since the young age of thirteen."

"Fifty-seven is also a young age. Do you mortals grow that much in such a short time?"

The queen's face tightened. "We do. Do you immortals value our customs so little that your refuse to wear clothes?"

"We do."

Pisces swept his newly-formed eyes over the queen. His skin was eons darker than hers and contrasted lovely with the hunks of white stone that made up the strange palace.

"Eh hem?" the queen asked with pinched lips.

"You mortals are always in such a rush." He sighed at the queen's lack of patience for the wandering thoughts that filled most of his time in the eternities. "And why should I make a deal with a mortal who slew one of my devout?"

The queen lifted her chin. "Because she failed."

"Hm." He grumbled, a coarse sound coming from his throat. He liked it. So he did it again. "Hm. Hm. Hm. That was not her fault. How could she succeed when asked to pull on my magic for one whom it is forbidden?"

"Why was your devout follower trying to give your magic to someone for whom it was forbidden?"

"Hm." He frowned, the muscles around his mouth curling downwards in a movement that took a surprising amount of effort. He raised and dropped them once more. "Fascinating."

"Great Pisces," the queen said, the skin on her face pinching together in a grotesque amalgamation. "Why have you withdrawn your magic from me?"

He let his lips be and set his galaxies upon her. "Because you serve my enemy and keep him trapped upon your ear."

Her eyes enlarged, little blue-rimmed stars gone sickly green. They darkened with black, and her lips quivered. "I do not know of what you—"

"Lies." He yawned, both irritated and horrendously bored with the whole situation. "You smell of Cancer and deceit when you emanate so dishonestly. Have you not been conversing with the Dreaded Kakkab for decades now? Feeding his insatiable appetite? Doing his bidding?"

She inhaled sharply.

"Hand him to me, and I will forgive you your debt and relieve you of your curse."

Her hand flashed to her earring, hiding the starry glow from his sight.

"Or," he added, the weight of his constellation in his voice, "you can remain forever barren. Now, decide."

CHAPTER TWENTY-EIGHT

Qadira

Qadira stared at the yellow diamond scimitar in Hulon's chest. Her mouth slipped open, words lost in the ferocious whip of the wind high up above the courtyard.

"Lahm?" she stuttered, at last, fixing her eyes to where he stood, bandaged and heaving.

The moonlight filtered across the palace ramparts and through his dark hair. His jade eyes shone in the dark, unadulterated by any one color.

He yanked the scimitar from Hulon's chest and collapsed onto his knees, throwing up in a heaving mess.

She rushed towards him.

"Stay back." He thrust a hand at her.

"But—"

"Stay back, please," he said, voice quivering.

She slowed, a chasm opening in her chest. "Lahm, I'm sorry."

He spat blood and hung his head low, hand still resting on the scimitar which stood on its point. He looked at her, voice low and shaking. "Did you kill Chiba?"

Crack.

Her heart froze. "What?"

"Did you kill Chiba?"

"I—" She fumbled, looking for the right words. The golden petals of the taluli nodded to her from the edges.

He raised his gaze to hers, an unfamiliar look of weary challenge in his glassy green. "It's a yes or no question, Dee."

Her nickname caught her off-guard. She swallowed. "Then... yes. But it wasn't what you think."

"And Icha?"

Crack.

"If you'll just listen—"

He stood and clanged the scimitar on the stone. "Yes or no?"

"Yes," she said but shook her head. "You weren't there. You didn't see. You don't know."

"Know what?" He raised the heavy blade and pointed it at her.

Dee looked down the diamond blade of his weapon, then at his clear eyes. The wind whipped. His scimitar held steady. Her breathing matched his, heavy and short, though it felt as if she couldn't breathe.

"Lahmdan..."

"I saw what you did to Nazdael!"

Crack.

"I saw you raise the mace. I heard it splatter, I heard her shriek as you pummeled our sister and shattered her bones. She didn't even fight back!" His green eyes seeped yellow, hints of black starring the middle. "How—How could you do that, Qadira?"

Her formal name on his tongue was worse.

Crack.

"Someone had to die," Dee whispered, the words newly foreign on her tongue. They were right, weren't they? They had to be... but it was hard to remember now.

"Is that what you said about Bruella?" Lahmdan accused. "Todor told me they couldn't even find her body, you must have destroyed her so thoroughly. Then burned it with Chiba to hide your brutality."

"That is not what happened!" Dee snapped, hurt poisoning her patience.

"You've snapped and gone mad. It's the only explanation."

Crack.

"I'm not mad. I was desperate. Alone." Qadira twitched, fingers aching to clench. "I thought I had already killed you."

He shook his head, over and over again, muttering under his breath. The point of his scimitar dipped. "Is this what you want?"

"Is what, what I want?"

"This?" He jabbed the blade out toward the view of Ahmar and the City of Pearls. "You want to rule? To be the queen?"

"No."

The nearest taluli opened and spat white mucus at her feet. She jumped back.

"Liar," Lahmdan's eyes narrowed. "You're always lying to me."

"Okay, maybe yes. But only because I want to rule with you, can't you see that?" She marched over to the edge of the rampart and grabbed a bushel of taluli and held them against her chest. "I want you to live more than anything." She waited, knowing the blossoms would stay closed. "See? I'm still your Dee Dee Ra. Your twin. I love you more than anything."

He stared for what felt like a full degree, the tiny Fourth Moon creeping up on the horizon as the First Moon fully set. The wind ruffled his hair. His scimitar dropped.

"Then why did you do it? How could you—" He choked. "How could you be so cruel?"

"I did it for you. Don't you see? I love you," she squeaked again, tightening her hold on the stems. "Lahm?"

He stared past her, out upon the city they killed each other for.

"Lahm, please. Say something."

He hates you.

"Liar," she hissed.

Lahm's brows furrowed.

"Shut up," she mouthed through the corner of her mouth.

Look at him. You disgust him now that he knows what you are.

She shook her head and pressed a hand over her right ear, her other cradling the taluli. "I'm not anything but his twin. His Dee De Ra."

That's not true. You're a witch. A murderer. And a queen. You've earned it.

"Quiet!"

Lahm's face contorted, a mask of confusion and a new tint of black clouding his eyes.

Fear. He was afraid of her. Just like everyone else.

Crack.

"I can fix this." she wrapped her arms around her stomach. "I can get him to understand. I just need to show him the truth."

"Who are you talking to?" Lahm snapped.

"My star. No, not my star. A star. I think he's a star." She grabbed the crystal drop and yanked it from her ear. "Here. He hasn't left me since you fell out the window."

Lahm grabbed the earring. He held it close to his face with furrowed brows. A swirl of mixed colors covered the jade in his eyes. He scowled. "It's just a piece of crystal, Qadira."

"Stop *calling* me that," she snapped. "Not you. And no, it isn't. He talks to me. He gives me weapons." She swallowed hard, chest tightening as the look on Lahm's face grew more worried, more worrisome. "He tells me to kill. He threatens you. He's behind so many of the deaths. So many horrible things. But he's also kept me alive when everyone else was trying to kill me. He's saved me."

Lahm scoffed, but his eyes drifted to the closed taluli. He rubbed his lip, then slipped his hand into his pocket, leaning back on his heels. "*Ya hasrety*, Dee," he groaned and pulled his hair with his free hand. "*Ya hasrety*, you're insane."

"It's true!" Dee growled. "Why do you think I did what I did to Nazdael? He was coming for you. I couldn't let him take you."

"You can't blame a crystal for your actions. Do you hear yourself?" He raised the earring.

"Lahm," Qadira yelped, reaching for it.

Then he tossed it over the side.

"No!" she screamed. She dropped the taluli and dove forward, snatching it before it fell and clutching it to her chest.

His eyes widened.

"It's not like that, Lahm." She reached for him.

He stepped back.

Crack.

"He will kill you if he gets out. I can't risk it. I have to keep him."

"You're either crazy or protecting a demon."

Crack.

Lahm ran his fingers through his hair over and over. "*Ya dahwety.* I don't know what to do."

"I'm not protecting a demon, I'm protecting you," she said. Her chest was beginning to numb, so great was the pain. Why wouldn't he believe her?

Because you're a monster. I wouldn't believe you either. Just save yourself and kill him like the rest to secure your rule. It is the better way.

"No!" she snarled, stomping on the taluli beneath her feet. She shot her gaze up to Lahm. "Stop looking at me like I'm a monster. I'm not. I'm your sister. We will rule together and I will always protect you, just like you said you'd always protect me. We won. We won it all. No one will ever hurt us again."

Lahm's face crinkled with disbelief, narrowed eyes yellow with horror. "Us?"

Crack.

"You and I." Qadira prompted, though it felt strange to say it now. "Like you said this morning. Like you said you wanted all along."

He cast his eyes down, then brought them slowly back up and thrust his hand out.

"What?" she asked, nerves pulled like a transgressor in the stocks.

"Give me the earring."

"Lahm—"

"Give it to me!" he bit, jabbing his hand at her. "If you want to rule with me, then rule with *me.* Just me. Not the demon who supposedly lives in that earring, whispering in your ear."

Qadira clenched the crystal in her sweaty palms. The wind whistled by in another strong gust that left her shivering. "I can't. It will get out. It will come for you. It—"

"It is trapped in an earring, Qadira, and in the locked and burned room before that. We can lock it up, too. Hide it away and be free from its evil."

Kakkab snickered in her ear, or maybe it was a growl. *He wants to see you weak, little queen. He wants you to be his shadow. To serve him after you did all the work. He never respected you now he wants to steal your power along with your throne.*

Qadira bit her lip, rubbing a thumb over the smooth crystal. "He's saved me. He gives me strength. He gives me power."

"So do I." Lahm pulled himself to his full height, squaring his shoulders. The night moons of Qaf shimmered against his outline in a soft glow. "Give me the earring, and we can rule together. All we need is each other."

Qadira looked between him and the star in her hand, its white light pulsing in the soft purple of her skin.

I won't stay trapped, princess. You know I won't. I'll whisper in his ear to kill you, instead. I only need one to live. So does Ahmar. And your people will never stand for you two ruling together. You will be forced to fight, in the end. Without me, who will win? Crying Qadira or the strategist who defied death?

Her fingers clenched tight.

"I can't, Lahm. It's... complicated."

Kakkab laughed.

Lahm hunched, face cresfallen, battering her heart.

"He's the only reason I live. I can't rule without him. I'll never make it."

"Little Dee... grown up in a day and completely unrecognizable," Lahm whispered.

His fingers clenched into a fist in his pocket, those of his other hand sliding over his face where they pinched the bridge of his nose. He took a shaky breath and straightened his shoulders once more. Then, he flashed his gaze to hers and grabbed her wrist. Green smoke enveloped them, and they apparated. In a moment, they were where they had started that morning, looking out at the courtyard from a window on the far janu'ub side of the Cyrstal Palace, just beneath the opening to King Malqum's bedchambers.

The taluli that previously lined the window were charred and withered, burned from the fire she had made for Bruella.

Lahm dropped her hand and met her gaze. "I didn't want this."

Her pulse hammered in her ear. It felt naked and cold, so she slipped Kakkab back upon her ear, both ashamed and desperate to keep him with her. "Want what?"

He sighed, slow and long. Then looked up at her with copper shining in his eyes. Bravery. Her breath stopped, and her throat closed tight. Why?

His lips curled in a hard look she had never once seen blemish his beautiful face. He grinned, setting her nerves aflame.

"You turned out far different than I expected, I'll admit that."

Crack.

"Lahmdan," Dee's voice trembled, "what are you talking about?"

"I'm talking about your performance. Sure, I had to help with the final two, but you made quick work of the rest. I wasn't expecting that."

Crack.

"No," Qadira stuttered, then tried again, defiant. "No. You were dead. You fell out the window and barely lived."

He nodded and shoved his hand in his pocket, his once-comforting smile a betrayal with teeth. "You're not wrong. That was a terrible blunder. Even I forget how much of a clutz you are. When I started the Allaedam with Ma's death, I wanted to watch your descent into murder and mayhem, but all I got was hearsay and a headache."

Crack.

"I'm not murderous. Or...I never wanted to be. I did what I had to to survive." Dee punched her thigh. "But I won't have to kill anymore. See? No weapons." She held open her empty palm.

Then his words fully sank in.

"What do you mean *when* you started the Allaedam?"

Lahm shrugged.

Ice burst from her heart and shattered her veins. "You lied."

"Ma was going to die either way. Why wait for a random day when I didn't have time to prepare? It was better to trigger it and be ahead of the game."

Crack.

"You said you wanted to rule together."

"I said what you needed to hear to be on my side. Why do all the work killing our siblings when they suspected I would try? It was easier to send you to do it."

Crack.

Her eye twitched. "But the taluli."

"You were too busy looking out the window to notice one spit on my shoe. When you took yours off to climb the wall in the courtyard, I realized you were brilliant. So I took mine off, too. You're far too trusting you know. Well, of anyone but yourself. You only ever watch the blossoms when you speak."

Crack.

"You said you wanted to rule together."

Lahm shook his head. "Not after what you've become."

"You made me this way. You started the Allaedam."

"And then you pushed me out of a window. Who's to say you didn't do that on purpose?"

Crack.

"I didn't do that." She yanked on the loose hair around her face. "I didn't do that, and you said you love me."

"I loved my sister, sweet, naive little Dee. Now, you're a murderous, monstrous, glittering queen with five jewels for your crown. Your face has grown so cold it could never be a mirror of mine. Thank the Bahamut for that."

Naive. Monstrous. Glittering not sweet. Not a sister or a twin. A murderous queen.

But not even that.

And after all that she had done. After Icha and Chiba. After Nazdael. Green flashed from eyes, lighting the palace walls.

Qadira's open palm cinched shut.

A twisted dagger with a triangle point appeared, a deep black that reflected no light.

Lahm's eyes widened. So did hers.

He raised his scimitar.

"No. You don't understand." She threw the knife out the window, but before it could clang on the cobblestone below, it reappeared in her hand.

Twice more she tossed the knife, wanting to rid herself of the murder growing angrily in her heart, but it clung to her skin like Nazdael's sparkles, her blood.

"Kakkab!"

Silence.

"Stop talking to yourself!" Lahm bit. "A shadow shouldn't talk at all."

Crack.

She tightened her jaw. "Don't call me that."

He pointed his scimitar at her chest. "What? Qadira? Or the shade that exists behind me when I face the First Moon? A figment that can't exist without me. Do you know why everyone called you a shadow? Because I told them you were one, first."

"Stop it!"

"Little Dee Dee Ra killed her twin and went crazy," he continued. "That's what they'll say. She killed him and started talking to his ghost, thinking it was some star in her ear. Then killed all her siblings in a delusional rage."

Crack.

She gnashed her teeth, and the dagger grew warm in her hand. "You are not a ghost. The star is real."

He laughed.

She snarled.

"There's only one way to know for sure. Let's fight and find out. Just you and me, not your stupid star."

Kill him. Kill him. It's the only way to know.

Her grip tightened.

"You don't know what you're saying," she gagged. "How could you say that?"

Because he despises you for your power. He wants you as his shadow. His nothing. He can't be trusted. He wants you dead so he can wear you as a jewel in his crown.

"That's not true," she hissed. "It can't be."

Lahm smirked. "You're doing it. Again. Who are you talking to this time? Me or me?"

She dropped the dagger to pull her hair and hit her scalp with the hilt when it reappeared. "Stop it!"

"Either I'm a ghost or you are. Whose body really hit the cobblestones? Yours or mine? Whose will this time? Is this a dream or have you transformed into a monster?" He pointed his sword at her chin and smirked. "Fight me and figure out if you're crazy or not."

Yes, kill him. Kill me. Kill someone, little queen. Dust more blood with your shining glister.

"I can't!"

One of you must die.

Crack.

"You love me!"

Crack.

Lahm sneered. "I don't."

Crack.

"You must!"

Red.

Crack.

Black that sucked away the light.

Crack.

And too much glitter.

Crack.

She screamed and struck.

ASCENDANCY OF QUEEN QADIRA

A FORMAL DECLARATION

BY THE GRACE AND providence of the Celestial Bahamut on the thirty-fifth day of the Seventh Moon's Thousandth Shadow Pass, in the time of the Fifteenth Allaedam to secure the throne of Ahmar, the Eighth True Heir, Qadira, has proven her worth and commitment to the throne through the deaths of six True Heirs and shall Ascend.

Long live Queen Qadira!

CHAPTER TWENTY-NINE

The Queen

Qadira froze, the air in the palace crystalizing in her lungs. The entire court seemed to hold their breath with her. All but Pisces, the mighty Star of Life, who picked at his nails. He was twice as tall, twice as attractive, and twice as flippant as anyone in the room. She hated everything about him, but it was the ultimatum he had made her that set her fire ablaze.

You can't be serious, Kakkab hissed in her ear, his voice barely above a whisper. *After all I've done, you'd just hand me over to that pretentious oaf?*

She bit the tip of her tongue, forcing composure in bones that wanted to tremble, and whispered, "I thought you wanted to be free. Maybe that's what Pisces wants with you. To let you go."

Kakkab coughed a bitter laugh. *Pisces will not free me. That cantankerous constellation is not a fan of mine.*

"Is anyone?" she asked, her stomach twisting like a knife.

She wanted to chew her lip, but that would smear her makeup. She wanted to bow her head but that would topple her crown. So she kept her face placid and stared at the Celestial instead, a picture of composure and anything but. Her entire court looked upon her, eyes as wide as the day Lahm fell from the window.

The corner of her mouth twitched.

She addressed the room, her words ringing out across the tile. "If you speak a breath of this meeting to anyone, I will slit your tongues and drown your children in your blood. Now, get out! Everyone but the star."

The courtroom cleared in an instant, courtiers, servants, and guards all tripping over each other to get out.

When silence filled the room, she spoke. "Do you know what I've given to keep my star?"

Pisces waved his mortal hand. "I don't care."

"You—" She chomped her teeth shut and swallowed the rest. "Why do you want him?"

"Because he's a bringer of death, of course. Why do you want him?"

Yes, little Dee. Remind me what I've done for you.

Qadira's jaw quivered. "He is the reason I live."

Pisces laughed a bubbling chortle that verberated in her mind and joints. "Kakkab is only capable of death, you foolish mortal. It is why your kingdom is soaked in it. What's the real reason you keep him by your side? Too afraid to kill djinn on your own? Need him to hold your hand?"

Kakkab snickered.

Qadira seethed.

"You mortals are all the same." Pisces rolled his eyes and scratched his exposed stomach—a perfect washboard of the deepest black. "You pretend you're strong and powerful, and then make our magic do all the dirty work. Can you even kill someone without the Star of Death on your ear?"

Excellent question.

Her throat tightened.

"Have you ever?" His lips slackened into a sloppy sneer. "Or are you Kakkab's little shadow?"

A figment that can't exist without me... Now, where have I heard that before?

"Enough!" Qadira spat, scalding rage broiling in her chest. She clenched her fist, wanting, as always, to kill the star who lived in her head. "Take him if you want, but you must kill him immediately."

Traitor!

Light flashed through the stars dotting the Celestial's body, blinding her temporarily. His voice shook the throne room. "Do not command me, mortal. Kakkab is mine to do with as I will."

"Then I refuse to hand him over." She straightened her spine and looked at him with the defiance of a star

More rays of light shot from the constellations in his skin. His whole body shook and trembled.

After all I've done, you'd sell me off to a star who would see me dead.

She narrowed her eyes. "Can he only get you if I sell you off?"

Kakkab went silent.

She smirked. "It's as I suspected," she raised her voice to the eternal being in the room. "A Celestial law holds you back, doesn't it? For whatever reason, you can not take Kakkab from me. Otherwise, you would have done so already and burned me to ash."

Pisces' skin bubbled as if a river of magma flowed beneath. "You dare command the Star of Life to end another's? The insolence. By doing so, I would be ascribing to the acts of my very enemy, whom you wear on your ear like a frivolous trinket."

"I cannot in good conscious allow you to release a being who will slay me as soon as they are free."

And I will, you treacherous witch. I will wring your neck a thousand times before I accept your life as punishment if you hand me over to that pompous, pious, putrid Pisces.

She took a step toward Pisces and away from Kakkab's snarled threats. "I'm no shadow, Celestial. I will be respected. I will only hand him over if you swear that I shall be free of my debt and that you will provide me and my posterity safety from the retribution of the Star of Death. I demand it."

"Demand of me—"

Bleeding bipedal, I'll kill you for this. Piece of piss Pisces. If you hand me over to him, I'll destroy that ball of gas and then come here and slit everyone in your kingdom's throat and wash your glitter off in their blood.

She smirked, feeling powerful all on her own for the first time... ever. Maybe she didn't need Kakkab after all. Not when she could make both Celestials so upset so easily. She held all the pieces here.

Qadira took another step toward the Celestial. "Or we can take a risk and see what happens. I wonder who your eternal enemy will punish first? He's not happy you're here for him in his weakened, trapped state. He can be so dramatic. But you know stars. Anyway, someone must die, the Star of Death demands it, and it has always been so. The question is, will it be you, him, or me?"

"I will not kill him!" Heat flared from Pisces, shredding his skin in beams of white that blasted columns and shattered holes in the crystal dome overhead. Glass tinkled to the tile around them.

You play a terrible game, queen, and for it, we may both perish.

Qadira's confidence wavered.

Pisces smashed his djinn teeth together, the rays of heat returning to bubbles under his frothing skin. He took a visible breath, his whole body shaking and bubbling. "I will grant you life in your womb and promise you indemnity from the actions of Kakkab."

The queen smiled, her teeth glittering like a constellation. "I accept."

Pisces snarled and held out his shining hand.

The queen looked at his palm, her boldness suddenly diminished. She had made the offer in anger, just like she did everything else, but she had not been without Kakkab for forty-four years. She hesitated, hoping he would throw a barb her way, something to incite her rage and help her do the hard things she never could. But he was silent, silent and sulking, surely betrayed by her actions. But she was queen, not him. She shone like a star, she did not hide behind them. And the last time she had chosen Kakkab, she had lost her family. She would not do that again. It was her last chance to find another djinn who would love her despite everything. If no one else could, her child surely would.

She gently pulled the crystal from her ear and dropped it in his hand.

Pisces laughed, hysterical and rumbling. He held up the crystal and watched the magic swirl inside. Then yanked it closer to his eyes. "What's this?"

Another rough sound ripped from his throat. White rays shot in every direction, melting the walls wherever they touched. The queen screamed and threw herself out of the way.

"What is this?" he yelled, voice booming with the force of the cosmos. "You give me The Goose? Do I look like a fool?"

"The Goose?" the queen stuttered, cold filling her up.

Silence.

She clenched her fist. "He is Kakkab. He has declared himself so for all the time I've known him. Rumors say he disappeared two centuries ago, the same time as when he laid fire to King Malqum's chambers and killed them all. He murders. He kills. It must be him."

Pisces held the crystal to his ear, his scowl deepening. "All I hear is the pathetic whisperings of Anser, The Miserable. Anser has killed no one. How could he when he was trapped in this crystal cage? Not that he would otherwise, that pathetic being delights in having others stir up chaos for him. You did it, as his devout."

Silence.

"He kills without me." Qadira crawled to her feet and stumbled forward. "He kills indiscriminately. Little Chiba, I did not—" Her eyes widened, and she grabbed at her hair. "I did. But he said—"

"Lies," Pisces finished her sentence. "Anser is only lies. Mischief. Madness. Chaos. All of these. But the power over something as absolute as death? Ha!"

"No!" The queen charged at Pisces and fell back just as quickly, rays of his power disintegrating the white stone beneath his feet. She screamed. "Kakkab"

But the horrible eternal being whispered nothing.

Her eyes darted up to Pisces. "No. He said to kill or be killed. He said someone must die. Someone always died!"

"At your hands, not his," Pisces shook his djinn head. "You are as wretched as he is."

"Kakkab!" She fell to her knees and lifted the crown from her head. "Anser, you demon! You told me they had to die. You told me he was going to. All those things, I did... All those djinn I killed!"

She rose to her trembling feet, jostling the crown, so the ornate headpiece glistened with its thousand tiny crystals and six large diamonds, each with the ghost of memory attached. Then she smashed it at her feet. Sparkles shot across the floor, tinkling to stop in chaotic disarray. Shattered. Useless. Like her mind.

"I would pity you, stupid queen, but you're insufferable. You will pay your debt to me by wearing The Goose in your ear until the day you die." He threw the earring at her feet. "And never call on me again."

"But my baby," she reached out, hollow desolation pouring from her voice and smearing her soul.

"Shall never be," he spat. "And good riddance to a kingdom that rules by death."

Qadira fell to the ground and scooped up the earring, its warmth a curse on her skin, and screamed.

CHAPTER THIRTY

LAHM

LAHM LAY GASPING FOR breath in the halls of the palace he had traversed freely in his short thirteen years of living. His lungs hurt. His foot did. Every muscle and bone in his body ached as if it had died falling from a five-story window and been brought back to life, only to be stabbed seven times and die again.

Qadira had left shortly after his body had stopped twitching, though the light had not yet faded from his eyes. She didn't want to look at him, the brother who had said such terrible things. That was okay. He understood.

Drowning in pain, he tried to move as little as possible. Blood filled his throat, desperation his heart.

Breathe, little djinn. I am here.

He gurgled his reply—not words, just thanks that he was not alone, even though he was. He had lost everything, everyone. His family, his laughter, his life. But worst of all, he had lost his best friend. His sister. His twin. His little Dee.

It is a noble thing you did. The eternities will remember. Though I still don't understand why you did it. I could have saved you, too.

"Only—" he choked and swallowed the burn of djinn fire and blood. "—one."

Then I could have saved just you. Not the terrible queen who has fallen to Anser's tongue.

Lahm shook his head and spat out a wet cry. "Meant to be." He shuttered as agony stabbed at his lungs. He paused, panting, hurting, missing her. Then a question struggled to the surface of his mind. "Will Anser leave her now? Please—" He sputtered a sob, and tears leaked from his cheek. "Please, say she'll be free."

That is up to your sister. Anser must bring order to find his freedom, and I don't see that in your ferocious queen. He has done what he always does and driven her mad. But she may find her way, yet. It is her choice, you see.

Lahm forced a small nod. The edges of his vision blurred, light and dark vying like shadows in his mind. "You?"

I have fulfilled my debt twice, first by saving you and then letting you die so she could live, instead. I wait only for you to fulfill your promise to me.

Lahm mustered his remaining strength and bent his elbow. His hand slid across the rough floor until it found his pocket. Pain seared his veins as he pulled the earring from his pocket and slipped it into his mouth. "One more," he groaned around the crystal orb.

What will you have of me?

"Keep her safe. Don't—Don't let her die. Give her time—" *To change*, he wanted to say. To grow. To heal. To find someone to love her once again. But the thoughts were lost in the swirl of dark and light that grew closer, blotting out all else.

As you wish, little being. Close your eyes and rest, and I will stay here and watch over her until she passes at the time of her choosing. Then, I will take you both with me.

Lahm closed his eyes, remembering her smiles and laughter, how she chased him through the halls and spared the little rams. He had done all he could for his sister, for Qadira, for his sweet little Dee. And he believed she was more than she could see. She was good, he knew it, and she'd find herself again, he just knew she would.

Satisfied with the hope of her future, he summoned his final surge of strength and bit the earring, letting Kakkab free.

EPILOGUE

The Baby

El Anaaji held her little baby close to her chest. Every little breath made her tummy squeeze. He was perfect and beautiful, his dark maroon lips soft like hers and his eyes orange like his father's. He cooed, and she nuzzled his nose in thanks for the little love note to her heart.

Qadira's screeches dashed the feeling upon the bitter rocks of reality.

"How much longer do you think I must scream?" She threw herself back upon her pillows with a huff. "I'd like to show him off already."

El Anaaji tore her eyes away from her sweet child and to the spoiled queen. Qadira was the least bedazzled she had seen her since a child. Her clothes consisted of the standard white muslin, the midwives insisting glitter was harmful to the baby. Her crown had been set aside, ominous and threatening on a cushioned table in the corner. Her hair hung in simple braids and her lips were bare. The only thing that glimmered on her body was a crystal earring that hung from her ear.

It took a great deal of effort to keep her temper back, but El Anaaji had known this day was coming long before. She inhaled deeply and released her breath slowly.

"I labored for eight hours, you've only been pretend laboring for two."

Qadira groaned. "So we'll just say I'm faster than most. I do everything sooner anyway, including ascending to the throne. Midwife Yana will corroborate my story, won't you?"

She looked for confirmation from the head midwife, who nodded, her face a crumpled mess of frustration since Qadira had forced her compliance in the charade eight months ago. Hers and that of two other healers. The only other people in on the deceit were Pardaj and El Anaaji. Though that was her fault. She should have known what her sister was up to the second she said *wide hips.*

But the truth remained. When El Anaaji had signed a debt of life to Qadira that fateful day during the Allaedam, she hadn't expected it to be repaid like this. She and Qadira had been entirely different people back then, shadows of what they were now.

Which is how, after securing the meeting with the Pisces—a gargantuan feat all on its own, though Qadira had yet to thank her even once—she had been sent to fetch the Ghaluman chieftain.

Pardaj had resisted with a bit of sass, but she refused to take no for an answer. There was an altercation, then an ultimatum. Fight the khanaziri pigrats and win, and he would go. She was about to jump into the pit of snarling desert beasts when a *tset aldhayle* arrived with a letter from Qadira. In addition to bringing the warlord home for marriage, she was also to bed him and become pregnant with the next heir to Ahmar's throne.

She had balked at first, but the Ghaluman was a specimen, indeed. Built like a drakonte, all muscle and sinew, with a smile that could melt the ancient frost on the Zabriyan mountains. He had laughed at the proposition, but when she put a blade to his throat and dared him to insult her again, he had practically purred.

It was play after that. A drink of water after thirsting in the desert. A spark of light in eternal darkness. In short, it was pure, unadulterated fun.

And even though she didn't know how she knew the second he had growled and she had yelped, both entangled in strange-found pleasure, that his seed took. Her body was strong, the heir would grow. As long as she stayed away from the throne and kept her head down, her debt was repaid. She was free. And the next day, he would marry the queen and rule, all for agreeing to sleep with her sister and keep his mouth shut, too.

El Anaaji ignored Qadira's grumblings and looked down at her precious babe. It was okay that he was coming to live in the palace that had haunted her growing up. There could only be one heir, and this time, there would be. From the beginning.

She would die before she gave Qadira another heir, and no other sibling lived to pass on the royal flame. Her baby would be free, free and happy. At least, she hoped.

Qadira whined, high-pitched and nasally. "I'm tired of waiting. You've been holding him since we snuck you in here. Let me have a turn."

El Anaaji bristled. He was not some toy or knife to be passed around so carelessly. He was also not hers. Not in a way he would ever know.

She bit her cheek. "Yes, my Queen." She stood and walked over to the bed. With a final kiss on his chubby little cheeks, she let him go.

Qadira scooped him into her arms, her bony elbows the only cushion for his head. She looked awkward as ever but determined to succeed. There was comfort in that, even if it was small.

"What's his name?" Qadira asked, looking up at her.

El Anaaji smiled. "Arash."

"Meaning?" Qadira narrowed her eyes, probably deciding if she would fulfill the promise she had made to let her sister name him.

"Bright." *And truth*, though she kept the second half to herself.

Qadira pinched her lips, then smiled. "Acceptable." She scrunched the baby in for a quick hug and beamed—the first look of joy El Anaaji had seen on her face since Lahm died. "Now," Qadira looked up at her. "Get out."

Arabic Phrases

'ana asf - I'm sorry

Eahira - Whore

Faqayd - Deceased

Hakim - Wise

Hamam - Bath

Huraasi - Guards

Jamila - Beautiful

Mahbub - Lovely

Murabae - Squire

Takun ealaa alsalam - "Be at peace"

Whakim - Man

Ya dahwety - An expression of woe

Ya hasrety - "Oh my heartbreak" that denotes a mournful sense of loss, disappointment in opportunities, or dashed hopes, all tinged with an underlying ache of sadness.

Qafian Terms

Arak Hunak - A virgin-eating tree that serves the goddess Cybele.

Famels - A disease that afflicts djinn similar to a mix between smallpox and leprosy.

Hitchwitch - A savory pink herb that possesses the magical ability to speak to the divine and is often used by witches to commune with stars.

Marleki - A crow-like bird that has sharp teeth and red eyes and lives in the swamps of Izrak. Feasts on human flesh and is often seen as a sign of death.

Paneena - Desert bug with pink gossamer wings that melt in water.

Quwian Seeds - The seeds of the Quwian tree. They are highly explosive and found only in Izrak.

Sansaazi - A bright yellow bird that inhabits the temperate woods of Ahmar. Rare and hunted mercilessly for their incredibly soft feathers that can be imbued with magic and that are used for anything from bedding to signage pins.

Yetollamae - Shrub with purple leaves and yellow flowers that bloom in Ahmar's equivalent of summer.

Djinn Eye Color Guide

Black: Fear. Mist swirling in the eyes

Blue: Hope, Anticipation

Green: Jealousy, Envy

Purple: Sadness, Grief, Despair

Gold: Happiness, Joy

Pink: Anxiety, Nervousness

Red: Lust. Glows in pupils

Silver: Compassion, Commiseration

White: Shock, Surprise. Lines like lightning

Yellow: Disgust, Disdain, Loathing

Orange: Embarrassment, Humiliation

Copper: Confidence, Bravery, Pride

Brown: Malice

Gray: Awe, Amazement

Eyes are Clear: Honesty, Forthrightness

Eyes flash with bright light: Anger

Colors do not match what is being said: Deceit

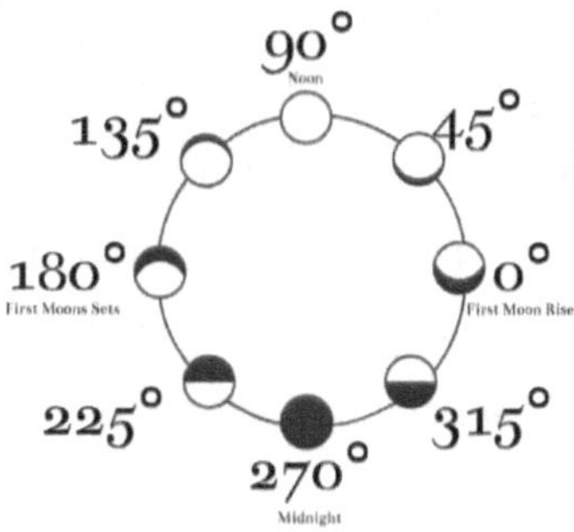

Time

Time is measured in degrees based on the orbit of the First Moon. One degree is equal to roughly four minutes. And 15 degrees is roughly one hour.

The First Moon:

A rough, rusty sphere of copper. The First Moon is the largest and brightest of the eight, taking up a full eighth of the sky when it is full. The path of the First Moon is the Qafian equivalent of 'daylight' and it is their main means of telling time. It comes up in the sharq and sets over the Bahamut Sea.

The Second Moon:

Quick-moving silver moon that passes through the sky about ten and a half times every 360 degrees. This moon follows the first moon, rising sharq and setting bahamut.

The Third Moon:

Pale pink, this moon crosses the sky perpendicular to the first moon, bouncing back and forth as it chases the swish of the Bahamut's tail. It rises janu'ub/gharb to shamaal. It is common lore that the Bahamut's former lover lives on this celestial body, pulling and yearning for its true love and creating the Qafian tides. The position of the third moon is preferred for telling time because it is always visible except for when it dips behind each horizon.

The Fourth Moon (Lover's Moon):

A dim yellow, this moon is nearly impossible to see when the First Moon is out and is sometimes called the "night moon". It only shines brightly during Qaf's *night*. It is often referred to when saying people are up to no good because only criminals, ne'er do wells, and lovers stay up late enough to see the Fourth Moon.

This moon passes twice for every single pass of the First Moon, once during Qaf's day unseen, then once through Qaf's night when visible. This moon rises sharq/shamaal to bahamut/shamaal.

The Fifth Moon (Witch's Moon):

The witch's moon of soft green that passes through the sky five times, following the Five Winds and crossing the sky 45 degrees (or 3 hours in Ard equivalence) at a time (with another 45 degrees to pass over to the other side beneath Qaf). It starts sharq and crosses to bahamut, then rises in janu'ub and sets shamaal, then rises gharb and sets sharq, then inverts and rises bahamut and sets janu'ub, then rises shamaal and sets gharb, then rises sharq and sets bahamut, like it started. This follows a 405 degree (or 27 hour)/27 day pentagon cycle and is difficult to track. It is the fortune teller's moon as they track its erratic behavior through the heavens and is often associated with Saqueia and the 5 Winds.

The Sixth Moon:

A soft-white moon that crosses the sky three times, 30 degrees after the rise of the First Moon, 60 degrees after midday, and at midnight. It travels from janu'ub to shamaal on each pass. It is the easiest moon to tell time by, has a medium heat, and most resembles Ard's moon.

The Seventh Moon (Shadow Moon):

This moon appears in odd years as a black circle in the sky that blots out the stars but does not give off any of its own light or heat. It takes an entire year to pass over the sky, and then is gone for an entire year. The measurement of Qaf's year and the seasons are determined by the movements of this moon.

It rises sharq/shamaal and sets gharb, dividing the upper and lower continents. It separates them but also forces them to look toward each other whenever they look at it and reminds them they share Qaf. Wars take place more often in the year this moon is hidden. It is also believed by some that it gives off no heat or light because it is the servant of a celestial that is dead or away or because the celestial they serve is.

The Eighth Moon:

A rare bright blue moon that only rises once every thirteen years—The Festival of the Eighth Moon. It rises janu'ub and sets bahamut/shamaal, rising directly behind Fyre. Every 130 years the appearance of the eighth moon will coincide with every other moon being visible in the sky. This is the "Festival of the Eight Moons," Qaf's most important holiday as it only comes once in most djinn's lifetimes.

It is the warmest moon, and Fyrans believe it serves the Origin, gaining its power from beneath Qaf like lava and only appearing rarely as a reminder to Qaf that the Origin is equal in power to the Bahamut, Celestials, and other minor deities.

The Moonless Night:

Every fourteen cycles of the First Moon in a shadow year of the Seventh Moon comes The Moonless Night, when all of the Eight Moons of Qaf are hidden beyond the horizon. During this time, all heat is sucked from the land and the stars shine their brightest. It does not last the whole night.

ABOUT AUTHOR

KYRO DEAN

Kyro Dean has written over 20 novels, including The Baron's Ghost, which can be found on Kindle Vella. In addition to her works for Eight Moons Publishing, she owns and edits for the blog, Vanilla Grass Writing Resources. She loves to speak and present and has shared her knowledge at many conferences. When not writing, she loves spending time with her delightfully curious children and talking with her plants, though they often give terrible advice.